Entangled

Book 2
Serendipity Adventure Romance

Anna Lowe

Editing by Lisa Hollett

Cover design by Fiona Jayde

Contents

Free Books

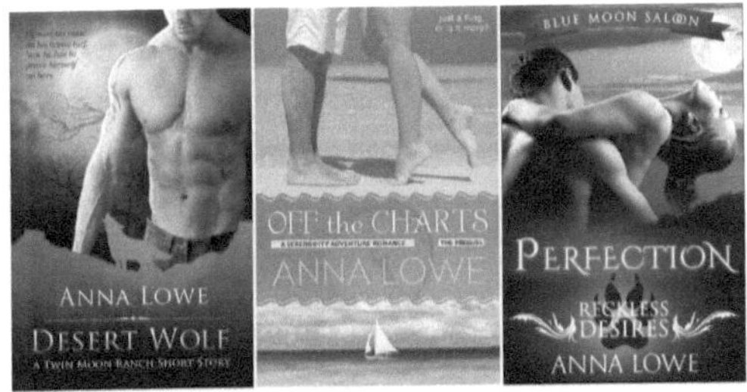

Get your free e-books now!

Sign up for my newsletter at *annalowebooks.com* to get three free books!

- *Desert Wolf*: Friend or Foe (Book 1.1 in the Twin Moon Ranch series)

- *Off the Charts* (the prequel to the Serendipity Adventure series)

- *Perfection* (the prequel to the Blue Moon Saloon series)

Chapter One

There was no way this could be the right bridge.

No way.

Tobin looked left, then right, but it was just him there. Him and his motorcycle in the middle of five hundred square miles of rain forest, plus a creaky rope bridge hanging over a ravine. One of those made-of-vines, hang-on-for-your-life kind of jungle bridges you only see in movies or travel brochures.

Or Panama, fittingly.

The funny thing was, he'd come to this part of Central America picturing something entirely different. The Panama Canal. Surf breaks. Beach bars and coconut-husk drinks.

But there was a whole different side to Panama — the tangled jungle side, where jaguars prowled, tribesmen wore face paint, and only the fittest survived. Where rain fell in solid sheets — or so he'd been told. He'd managed to time things right for a change and come in dry season. More like dumb luck, because his timing, well, it always seemed to be a little off.

He cut the engine, swung off the bike, and tried the first of the wooden boards that formed the ramp of the bridge. Solid enough.

He gripped the handholds on either side and took another step. At least there was that: the bridge only looked like it was made of spit and vines. It was actually made of spit and thick wire. Rusty wire, judging by the smudge of orange on his palm.

But hell, life was for living, even if it meant risking your neck from time to time. He took another couple of steps out, edging away from firm land and out over the ravine. The

1

bridge was barely a yard wide, but it stretched on and on across the gorge, a thin sliver squeezed into a lush green jungle that seemed to have no beginning and no end.

The farther he ventured, the more the roar of the river filled his ears, and the more the bridge wobbled and bounced. The footboards were slippery and beginning to rot, and it was all too easy to imagine putting a foot right through one and plunging into the rushing river, a hundred empty feet below.

Probably not the best place to stop and swing his backpack off to pull out the camera, but he just couldn't pass up the chance. He held on with one hand and turned the camera around for a selfie.

Another great shot for his *Adventures in Central America* album, if he ever got around to making one. Another shot he'd probably never let his mother see. And another picture of him in an amazing place, alone.

He snapped another few shots, trying to get the motor-cycle in the background, because he'd made it clear across Central America on that thing. Too bad he'd left his machete strapped to the saddlebags, because that would be the ultimate picture to send to friends back home. He could imagine what his friends back home might say — they of the eighty-hour workweeks, mortgages, and two-point-one kids.

"Tobin, man, keep living it up."

"We're living vicariously through you, Tobin."

"Now that's the way to live."

Of course, there were other opinions, too. The ones who asked when he was finally going to grow up. Settle down. Get serious about someone.

Which he might have been tempted to do, if he wasn't still in love with a woman he'd last seen six years ago. If she hadn't backed out forty-eight hours before they were supposed to say *I do*, who knew? He might just be living that suburban life. Enjoying it, even. Kissing the love of his life goodnight, every night.

He stared down into the ravine, watching the river tumble and split, each drop of water finding its own snaking path between the boulders. If the average guy was the mainstream, shooting down the middle of the river, he'd be the drop stuck over there in the back, swirling and tumbling and having a great old time. Not actually getting anywhere but right back where he started, ready for another wild, wet ride.

Good old Tobin, living it up. He sighed.

He looked up and found himself two-thirds of the way across. Veils of mist hung over the lush green landscape. A scar of a cliff opened a view of a waterfall that gushed in three uneven stages, but the rest was wild, tangled, and impossibly thick.

No sign of the village he needed to find. No sign of a road.

He rubbed a foot across the slippery footboard, and the rotting wood creaked. Time to turn around. He had a sense of adventure, not a death wish. And he'd wasted enough time. Somewhere out there was the right bridge, the right road. The one leading to the damsel in distress he was supposed to be rescuing.

He backtracked, wondering what was scarier: that he was her only hope, or the idea of seeing her again. Because the damsel in question wasn't the type to hang around waiting to be rescued, especially not by him. Cara was as likely to greet him with a right hook as a kiss.

So yeah, the odds of an epic fail were roughly ninety-nine to one. But hell, he lived his whole life in that one percent zone. Why buck tradition now?

And anyway, this was about her, not him. And definitely, definitely not about what they'd once had.

Definitely not? the back corner of his mind protested.

He gritted his teeth. *Definitely not.*

Chapter Two

He spider-walked back to his motorcycle fast enough to make the whole bridge bounce up and down. Time to get to that village, wherever the hell it was, and get Cara out of whatever trouble she was in.

He'd barely set foot on terra firma when a wizened old man half hidden under a stalk of bananas appeared on the dirt road.

"*Hola,*" Tobin started. His Spanish wasn't great, but it worked. Mostly. "Tucumba?" He pointed across the bridge. "*Aqui?*" *This way?*

The man greeted him with a gap-toothed smile and a flurry of syllables. Tobin did his best to follow along. *Viejo* meant old, *nuevo* meant new, and *puente* meant bridge. The old man was pointing over Tobin's shoulder, which meant the new bridge was over there. It had to be, because if this was the new bridge — man, he'd hate to see the old one.

He fired up Lucy, the battered old 500cc Kawasaki he'd picked up in Belize, and rattled around a couple of potholes the size of a small Central American country.

Half a mile up the road, he spotted it: the new bridge. Wide enough for a jeep. High enough over the gushing river to make an alternative out of the question. Crumbling enough to make an engineer wince. And bristling with guards clad in fatigues.

Tobin eyed the scene from above, letting the engine idle.

The guards were heavily bearded Che Guevara-types, right down to the bandoliers, brown caps, and black leather boots. What were they guarding, sixty miles away from the Columbian border?

5

Guarding against drug runners, probably. A spike of heat rushed through his veins. What the hell was Cara doing up here, alone?

The guards weren't doing much guarding, though. They were all clustered around a tiny shack with their backs to the bridge, their focus inside. One of them shifted, and Tobin glimpsed a flickering blue light.

Television? Out here?

His eyes shifted higher, to the small satellite dish on the roof. Maybe it wasn't for strategic communications, but for entertainment. Which could only mean one thing.

Soccer. The World Cup was on, half a world away, and every man, woman, and child in Latin America seemed to be tuned in. He'd heard radios blaring all the way across the country. Some big game was on today.

And maybe, just maybe, that was his chance. Because there were two options for getting across that bridge: rolling up with a smile and submitting to the standard single-male-gringo treatment: a half-hour scrutiny of his passport, his bike, his pockets. Even then, they might not let him through. He'd heard a special permit was required to go this far into the jungle, and he had nothing.

Nada.

Zilch.

Which left him with option two.

Tobin eyed the bridge and the road that disappeared around a bend on the other side. He might just make it.

Might.

In any case, he didn't really have a choice.

Stuck in Tucumba, Cara's message had said. The one he'd received two days ago in an email from his cousin Meredith. An email that forwarded a whole series of messages that spun off from a short text from Cara.

Stuck in Tucumba, in the highlands. They won't let me out. Will miss my dead—

The message cut off there. Cara's parents were frantic — so frantic, that when they found out Tobin was in Panama, they wrote back right away.

Get Tobin! Get Tobin to help Cara now!

There wasn't a PS, but he could hear Cara's father muttering all the same. *And if the bastard fucks this up the way he fucked up everything else, he's dead meat.*

Yeah, her dad was a gem that way. A hard-working pizza parlor owner who probably had a distant connection to the mob — an Uncle Rocco who could wipe Tobin's ass off the planet with a single shot to the head. Never mind that Tobin's name had once been embossed alongside Cara's on a wedding invitation. These days, he was persona non grata. They were only making a temporary exception because he was the closest one.

He gunned the engine and rattled along the single-track road, slaloming between ruts and dips that would have torn the bottom out of most four-wheel drives.

Will not fuck up. Not this time.

The road dipped downhill so steeply, the back wheel left the ground with a lurch that echoed in his gut. He sped around a bend to the approach to the bridge.

His eyes flicked briefly from the ruts in the road to the guards. Still focused on the game.

Back to the road, blurring under the front tire.

Back to the guards, closer now. His heart thumped in his chest.

The road straightened and Tobin opened up the throttle. The engine roared in his ears, but so did the river, and the guards didn't hear him.

Yet.

Then everything became a blurry rush as he zoomed right past them and onto the bridge.

"Argentina dos, Brazil uno!" the television commentator cried. *"Goooooooaaaaaallllll—"*

The goal celebration was drowned out by the shouts of the guards, who'd finally spun into action and reached for their guns. He could see them in the sideview mirror, now that the road was smooth. Smooth enough to hit another gear and gun it for the other side. A hundred feet and he'd be out of range, around the bend.

Eighty. The motorcycle flew off the lip of the bridge and back onto the dirt on the other side. He absorbed the impact with his elbows and knees and hung on for dear life.

Ping! He didn't hear the first bullet so much as felt it cut through the air.

Fifty feet to the bend. God, he hated being rushed.

A second shot rang out, and a third, then so many that he couldn't discern between the rat-a-tat-tats exploding all around him and the jarring of the bike. All he could do was duck — as if that did much good — and speed on.

Crunch! The sideview mirror shattered.

Crap. He'd just had that mirror replaced, too.

Thirty feet. The roar of the river subsided now that he'd reached the other side. The sound of bullets, though, grew louder. *Ping! Ping!*

Ten feet. He hunched over the handlebars and leaned into the bend with a hard twist on the throttle. And *zoom!* He was in the clear.

"Shit!" He jerked the handlebars right. The blind turn hid a half-gutted truck, raised on bare axles and a couple of logs. A wreck of a thing, but still solid enough to kill a motorbiker in too much of a rush. It loomed over him, and he tucked his elbow in tight. Cleared the wreck by an inch, and that was with half his weight stuck way out to one side. Raced on and told his heart to get the hell out of his throat and back to beating something steadier than a frantic bongo beat. Because he was fine. Absolutely fine, right?

He glanced back. The guards didn't seem to be taking up the chase. Not yet, anyway. The road was empty but for him, Lucy, and a startled old man with a reluctant mule. Tobin puttered past them and around a bend, then screeched to a halt, staring up. Straight up.

The engineers who built the bridge seemed to have called it a day there because the road petered out into a nearly vertical trail more fit for a goat than a four-wheel drive.

The man with the mule caught up with him. Tobin cut the engine and pointed up. "Tucumba?"

"Si, Tucumba." The man smiled and plodded on like there weren't a dozen guys likely to come sprinting around the corner any second. Like there wasn't raw, ragged jungle on either side. Like the love of his life wasn't being held captive somewhere up there.

"Tucumba," Tobin half muttered, half sighed.

Tucumba. If nothing else, there was kind of a high that came with living life this close to the edge.

Kind of.

He stashed Lucy as far off the road as he could. Which wasn't very far, considering the python-thick vines and tree roots. The jungle crept over the sides of the road, just biding its time before reclaiming stolen territory. The leaves of the nearest bush were each as big as an umbrella, and it didn't take long to hide Lucy. He slung his backpack over his shoulders, grabbed a water bottle from the saddlebags, and glanced back the way he'd come. No sign of the militia yet. If he was lucky, they'd already given up on him and gone back to the soccer game. If he wasn't lucky, well...

He took off, trotting up the mountainside.

Forty-eight hours ago, he'd been teaching beginner surfers off an endless sandy beach on Panama's Pacific coast. Now, he was sweating buckets and making like a soldier on some kind of marathon forced march. A Swiss soldier in an overgrown tropical version of the goddamn Alps. That's what it felt like after the first hour.

And the second, and the third. By which time he wasn't trotting, but trudging along. He might as well have poured the contents of the water bottle over his shirt for all that he was sweating now.

Sweating and swearing and slogging along. How the hell did Cara get to a place like this? Why? An image of her socked him so hard, he nearly stumbled. The first time they'd met, her coal-black eyes and long black hair made him think of a Roman goddess. The last time he saw her... Well, he'd rather not think about that.

Ahead, the trail narrowed to a footpath with solid walls of jungle on either side that were alive with a thousand unidentified squeaks, squawks, and screams. A monkey hooted. An angry bird fluttered right over his head. A giant purple-winged butterfly danced through a single shaft of daylight.

It was like a movie. Right up to the part when the bushes rustled. A swarm of brown shapes separated themselves from the shadows and surrounded him with a chorus of grunts.

Five compact, bronze men that barely came up to his shoulders. Five pairs of fierce eyes underscored by thick black paint lines. Bare chests, bare feet. Nearly bare everything, except for the loincloths.

That's not where he focused, though. The sight of five blowguns aimed his way was far more compelling. He gulped, picturing the poison-tipped darts inside, and stuck his hands up high.

"Um... *Hola?*"

Chapter Three

Cara stuck on a smile and wandered down the village path.

Maybe this time they wouldn't notice. Maybe this time she could get away.

Chickens scattered before her feet, and if she didn't raise her eyes too high, it might seem like any other village in any other Central American town — all familiar to her since accepting the job transfer to Panama two months ago. Barefoot children, pecking chickens, a dirt path. The quiet chatter of voices, the sound of women pounding grain over stone mortars. The mangy dogs, snoring in the afternoon shadows.

The minute she lifted her chin, though, everything changed. This wasn't like any other village she'd ever been, even in Panama. More like a photo spread in a *National Geographic* magazine, from the painted faces of the inhabitants to the thatched huts and thick jungle all around. The village was a tiny clearing in a vast carpet of living, breathing greenery. It might have been beautiful if she'd chosen to spend the last six days here.

But that hadn't been the plan. Not the plan at all. It was supposed to be a quick in-and-out visit — an afternoon of convincing an aging village chief to sign on the dotted line for a business deal he had no reason to turn down.

Except it hadn't gone that way. The meeting dragged on and on, and no matter what she tried, no one seemed willing to follow her script. Minutes stretched into hours, and when she finally emerged from the meeting house, shadows stretched over the ground and the guide who'd led her into this backwater had packed up and left.

"He what?" she'd yelped, first in English, then in Spanish, trying to keep her fiery Italian temper under control. "How am I supposed to get out?"

"Don't worry." Rodrigo, the chief's nephew, had just waved an indifferent hand. "We'll get you a new guide." He cleared his throat and mumbled. "Eventually."

Eventually?

She'd looked around for someone else to guide her out, but there was no one. Only the scowling French anthropologist who lived in the village, but he'd stomped away the minute she mentioned her company. No help there.

She'd really started to worry when a woman showed her to the cluster of tiny huts where the villagers put up ecotourists on the rare occasions someone wandered far enough off the beaten track to visit. Bird watchers. Butterfly enthusiasts or scientists of some kind.

But that night, it had been just her. The hut held a bed with a mosquito-net canopy, a basin and bowl for water, and not much else.

"*Buenas noches, señorita.*" The woman set a plate of food on the rough-hewn table, and then let herself out.

Buenas noches? Since when was she spending the night here?

Since five nights ago.

The jungle rose around the village like the walls of a prison, and the only way out was the road. She strolled down the village path, aiming her camera this way and that, trying to look like a tourist and not a jail-breaker as she edged toward the road. Or what passed for a road in this part of the world.

She'd made it as far as the second bend on the second day. Far enough for one bar to light up under the antenna symbol of her phone if she held it high in the air.

"Come on, come on." She'd coaxed the cell phone along. "Please, one more bar…"

The display flickered to two bars for an instant, then went back to none.

"God, please, just one message. Let me send one message. One little message…."

The signal had popped in and out, and she hit *send* each time, desperate to contact the outside world.

But then a gang of women had come along, clucking like a flock of hens and herding her back to the village. By the next day, it was obvious the villagers weren't just stalling, but downright refusing to let her leave. Every time she made a move for the road, they'd block her way. She even got up in the middle of the night and made a break for it, but the jungle noises had spooked her back into the village. The only thing she'd accomplished was getting out a backup message to her sister, if it went out at all.

She paused at a bush and pretended to sniff the pink blossoms, hiding her darting eyes behind the curtain of her long black hair. She sidestepped toward the road. Maybe today she'd make it far enough to get a signal, possibly receive a reply. Maybe she'd make it far enough to—

"Going somewhere, *señorita*?"

She whipped around so fast, her camera nearly clipped the man on the chin.

"Rodrigo." She narrowed her eyes on the proudest five foot four inches of tribal warrior she'd ever seen.

"A beautiful day in the village, no?" The chief's nephew stepped into her path, blocking the road.

The American English he'd picked up while studying abroad always caught her off guard, given his native garb. He spoke perfect English and Spanish, as well as the chirpy native language used here. The chief's nephew was a bridge between two worlds — one of those rare backwoods types who'd made it out into the big bad world before coming home to his roots. Cara could picture him picketing for indigenous rights in front of a courthouse, giving reporters catchy sound bites for the evening news.

She stuck her hands on her hips. "I was thinking it must be a beautiful day back in Panama City."

He scowled. "The city is never beautiful. No cities are. I've been there. I know. New York, Washington, Panama City: they're all the same." He shook his head. "It is only in the jungle that a person can truly breathe." His bare chest rose on a long inhale as if to illustrate his point.

"Rodrigo, I have to get back to work. Why don't you let me go?"

"Don't worry, *señorita*. On Sunday, you can go."

"Sunday is too late!" She had to present the plan to the national telecommunications authority on Friday at three. Without their okay, her company's plan was toast. Her job was toast.

"*Señorita*, enjoy the village. The beautiful rain forest. What they say in New York: kick back and relax."

She'd worked in New York for four years and had never met anyone who kicked back and relaxed.

"If I wanted to relax, I would have brought a change of clothes. A book. My diary." The one full of business deals gone right and personal things gone wrong. Badly wrong. "Rodrigo, why won't you let me leave?"

Rodrigo made a little sound that told her nothing. "Enjoy the village, *señorita*," he said and wandered away.

She plopped down on a log that served as a bench, kicked at the dirt, and spent the next quarter-hour contemplating her fate. She'd gotten one brief text out to work, but that was outside office hours. If the wrong person got to the messages first — like that skunk, Enrique, who'd been gunning for her job all along — well, who knew what he might be capable of. Such as conveniently hitting *delete*.

Somehow she had to get out, and soon. She had forty-eight hours to bust her way out of the back of beyond.

But how? She had a pair of sandals, a dying cell phone, and half a bottle of insect repellent. No Swiss Army Knife, no compass, no clue. She hadn't come to Tucumba for jungle adventures; she'd come to seal a deal. And Friday was only three days away!

A chicken pecked the dirt next to her foot. A rooster crowed for the fifth time in three minutes. He'd been going for most of last night, too, but she'd long since moved past fantasies of wringing his neck. She took an imaginary photo with her eyes for her mental album and scribbled a caption in: *The end of my career.*

The distant sound of voices filtered into her mind. They grew steadily louder — louder even than the constant background music of a thousand jungle insects chirping away. The excited chatter of half a dozen children filled the clearing, and she looked up. Someone was coming up the mountainside.

Two heads bobbed over the rise: one, a wiry old man who made the return trip every other day, and the other, his irritable counterpart, a mule loaded high with supplies.

Then a few more figures appeared behind them — a veritable crowd in this neck of the woods. A clutch of village men accompanied the old man, along with someone else. Someone taller, paler. The kids jumped down, blocking her view. It had to be an outsider, because who else could incite such a stir?

She stood up for a better look at the newcomer, trying not to hope too much. Maybe her company had finally sent someone for her! Maybe this was it — she could finally get out!

The minute she caught a glimpse of him, though, her knees wobbled and she sat down hard enough for her tailbone to cry in protest. But that was nothing compared to the wail coming from her heart.

Not him. Not now. Not here. This couldn't be happening.

"Gringo! Gringo!" The kids surrounded him like the messiah, and she could hear his good-natured reply.

"Hola! Hola!"

There was a happy lilt to his voice, which figured, because Tobin was kind and sunny and a kid at heart. Her girl parts were already fluttering in a Pavlovian reaction because they knew that voice, too. Intimately. It had been a long time since they'd last made love, but she could still feel him whispering into her lips, humming naughty promises in her ear.

The kids parted like the water in front of Moses, and there was Tobin, smiling and laughing like today was just another great day. Striding toward her like...like an Olympian stepping up to the podium to get his prize — and the look on his face said *she* was the prize.

Every signal in her brain scrambled; all her nerves fired at once. God, he was just the same. Same wave of thick brown hair that said he didn't give a damn how he looked — guaranteeing that he always, always looked like a girl's best fantasy. Same chiseled build, same sparkling eyes that said life was a champagne he could get drunk on, every morning and every night.

Six years and Tobin hadn't changed a bit. The blue of his irises danced, hinting at some joke he couldn't wait to share.

And yet he was different, too. Something about him was too bouncy, like he had to convince himself he was having a great time. The way his eyes cast around — not for an easy flirt, but for a friend.

She snorted. Lonely was not a word that fit in the same sentence as Tobin Cooper. The man drew women like grain drew geese, all of them squawking and preening and pecking one another the hell out of the way.

"Hi, Cara." His voice was even, but his chest heaved.

She opened her mouth but couldn't get anything out.

The chief's nephew broke in, jabbering at the men who'd brought Tobin in. He spoke in the local indigenous language, but the message was pretty clear. *What were you thinking, bringing this stranger here? How could you trust him?*

Tobin flashed Rodrigo a winning smile. *"Argentina dos, Brazil uno."*

She blinked. Was that some kind of code?

A ripple of recognition swept through the crowd, and a few even cheered. Soccer results? Sure, soccer was king in Latin America, and the smaller countries cheered Spanish-speaking Argentina over Brazil every time. But she hadn't expected these villagers to care.

"Who is this?" Rodrigo pointed an accusing finger as high as he could reach on Tobin's chest, which was at about the level of his pecs.

The flat, hard pecs she used to lay her head against before she fell asleep.

She gave herself a mental slap and forced her mind back into gear.

How Tobin had gotten here, and why — she couldn't figure out. But right now, he was her only hope.

Jesus Christ.

A crazy impulse of an idea rocketed through her mind and she sprang to her feet.

"Mi marido!" she squeaked, and only half that sound was faked. A second later, she threw herself at Tobin and smacked him with an openmouthed kiss.

"Marido! Marido!" The word went through the gathering villagers like a hum.

Electricity coursed through her as Tobin's hands cupped her waist. His lips twitched against hers, then pushed closer. She could taste the surprise there, along with the barest whisper of hope.

"Marido?" Rodrigo echoed, his voice dripping suspicion.

"Marido?" Tobin mumbled once she'd come up for air, gasping like a fish.

It wasn't often you caught a guy like Tobin off guard, and the look on his face was priceless. Except her words had caught her as off guard as they did him, and she was finding it hard to breathe.

"Marido." She nodded. "My husband."

Chapter Four

Tobin figured it would hurt to see Cara again, but it didn't. It just made his body sing.

His heart hammered from more than just the uphill climb. And the minute he spotted her, a whole chorus broke out in his soul, singing "Hallelujah" and "Crazy Love" and "Girl Be Mine." Every step in her direction was a step out of a dream — the one where she called to say she'd made a terrible mistake and begged him to come back.

Cara. The first person he'd ever met who made him want to do everything right instead of proving everything he could do wrong. The last woman he'd ever promised anything to. The only woman who made him want tomorrow as much as today.

"How'd you get here?" she hissed.

He shrugged. "The international language of brothership. Sports. Soccer." One minute they were aiming blowguns at him; the next, they were slapping his back and cheering. Crazy place, Panama.

"But what about the bridge?"

"What about it?"

"How did you get across the bridge?"

"Um..." He hesitated. It didn't seem like the best time to elaborate. "The usual way?"

He looked around. The men down at the bridge had walkie-talkies and machine guns. Up here they were small, bare-chested guys with loincloths and blow darts. Climbing that mountain trail seemed to have stripped centuries away.

But time didn't matter, not when it came to him and Cara.

"Husband, huh?" he managed once the roar in his ears settled down.

"Run with it, hotshot," she grunted in his ear.

His lips curled into a grin so wide, it hurt. She'd called him that on their very first night together, which came a couple of hours after they'd met for the very first time. Him, the ski instructor, thinking it was just going to be another frigid day in Vermont; her, the client, on a pair of skis for the very first time.

That day had been a dream, and that night... Wow. A prelude to what he was sure was destiny. The best thing that had ever happened to him: having her in his life. Preferably, forever.

She wanted him to run with the husband thing? He'd run with it, all right.

He closed his teeth over her right ear and gave it a tiny nip, just the way she loved. "Missed you, honey."

Which wasn't a lie. Not in the least.

Cara let out a tiny hint of a moan that put his cock on high alert, then and there. She shoved him away with a glare.

She was beautiful as ever, of course, with long black curls straight out of a portrait of an Italian princess, locked in a tower high on a hill. Coal-black eyes that glittered and shone, even in the slanting light of this mountaintop. Thirty years looked even better on her than twenty-four, and he couldn't keep from snuggling closer to her neck.

She stiffened. "Don't overdo it."

"It's true! I did miss you." Every day. Every night. He hid his nose in her hair for a minute, not to play the image up, but to hide. Because crap, it was totally true, and the truth made his eyes sting. It took a good dozen hard blinks before he could come up for fresh air.

She shot him a look before taking his hand and leading him away from the crowd. "I'll just show my husband where we're staying."

"Staying?" he whispered, making sure his lips got a good taste of her ear. "I thought you wanted to get out of here."

She looked at him, doe-eyed in wonder. "Is that why you're here? To help me?"

He picked his words carefully, because Cara didn't like to need help. "Meredith told me you were stuck out here. And so I came."

"From where?"

He wished he could say he'd dropped everything at his high-powered corporate job to jet down to Central America just for her, but hell, driving fifteen hours across the length of Panama had to be worth something, too. "Santa Catalina," he said. "On the Pacific coast."

"Catalina?" She gaped. "What were you doing there?"

"The question is, what are you doing here?"

Here being a twelve-by-twelve hut on the edge of the clearing in what looked to be a cluster of guest cabins set apart from the village.

"Hey! Wait a minute!" A wiry young man trotted up and stuck an accusatory finger at his chest. The man's eyes screamed jungle warrior; the black lines painted on his face angled with the frown he wore. Tobin expected a guttural indigenous language to come out of his mouth, but he spoke perfect English. "Who is this?"

Tobin stuck his hand out and flashed a huge smile. "Tobin Cooper. And you?"

The man's frown deepened.

"Tobin, this is Rodrigo, the chief's nephew," Cara said. It was more a sigh than an introduction. "Rodrigo, meet Tobin. And now, if you'll excuse us..."

Firm, polite, no-nonsense. Cara in business mode. Tobin smiled. The woman hadn't risen through the corporate ranks for nothing.

"Yes, if you'll excuse us." He put a little naughty in his smile. "I just can't wait for a little private time with my wife."

Cara froze with the door half-open.

Tobin pretended he didn't see. "It's been too long." Six years too long, but the guy didn't need to know that.

Her jaw clenched as she pulled the door the rest of the way out, and she motioned him in with a vicious swipe at the thick jungle air. A couple of curious kids had tagged along, and he peeled away gently and waved goodbye. "*Hasta luego,* kids."

The second he went in, his eyes landed on the four-poster double bed, draped with netting. Elegant, in a bush-camp kind of way. Suggestive, given the messy sheets. Like she'd just rolled him out of there instead of pushing him in.

Cara came in behind him, slammed the door, and the whole cabin shook.

Yep. It was Cara, all right. His Cara.

Chapter Five

He turned, squaring his shoulders. Cara was going to chew him out, he knew it. Let him have it for screwing everything up six years ago with one stupid act. Take all the frustration evident in her stiff body out on him. And he was ready to take it like a clueless puppy, because damn it, his imaginary tail was wagging wildly just to be allowed back in her life, even for a short time.

"So, your husband, huh?" he started before she could blow up.

"I was desperate."

"Clearly."

She glared.

"I did kind of like it, though." He risked a grin.

"You would."

"So, Mrs. Cooper, what brings you to—"

She batted his arm. "It's Leoni. Ms. Leoni." She drew out the *Mizz.*

"Coulda been Cooper," he teased. It was a reflex, like breathing. Blinking. Sleeping. Loving her.

And teasing. So much fun.

"I was going to keep my name, remember?"

Of course, he remembered. Loved her all the more for it.

"Then I could have been Leoni." He meant it as a joke, but his voice betrayed him and it came out all cracked and warbly. Sad. He covered up with a broad smile. That usually worked.

Not on Cara, though. She shook her head, and he braced himself for an onslaught. A full-on outburst of that Italian temper she unleashed every once in a while, with raging hands and fiery eyes and syllables that would come tumbling out on the end of a verbal battering ram.

Sure enough, she threw up her hands. "This is why we were never good together."

"We were always great together," he growled.

"You don't take anything seriously."

"You take everything too seriously."

"Marriage is a serious thing, Tobin. You shouldn't joke about it."

"It was never a joke." It came out in a rough whisper, and he covered up with a shrug. "You can joke or you can cry." A fine line he'd crossed more often than he'd care to admit.

She took a deep breath, then suddenly lost steam. Maybe she was listening, after all. Because she stood there with shaky hands and a shaking head, one breath away from falling apart — or slugging him.

Then her gaze caught on something on the right side of his face and she softened. Her hand cupped his cheek, and he closed his eyes to focus everything on the sensation of Cara, touching him again.

The rose petal scent of her filled his lungs. The soft pad of her thumb brushed over his cheek, and if it stung a little, he couldn't care less.

"What's this scar?" she whispered through quivering lips.

He didn't answer right away, because first he had to digest that proof. Cara noticed. She cared.

"Tobin?"

He was taking too long, but this minute might have to last him a lifetime, so he wanted to drag it out. The scar and the bruise that was still showing a little yellow after six weeks didn't matter. But it mattered to her, and that sent a flock of butterflies through his stomach.

"Tobin, what happened?"

Lying would be easier: he could say he got hit by a surfboard at work. But he'd never lied to Cara and wouldn't start now.

"Had a little run-in with the shady side of the law in Belize," he said and shrugged it off.

She looked at him with such big eyes, looking uncharacteristically fragile and full of regret.

"Cara," he started, but she held up her hand in a stop signal and closed her eyes.

Okay, not a time to talk. But maybe a time to hold. He stepped over to her and wrapped his arms around her, nowhere near as abruptly as she'd hugged him outside but just as tightly. Listened to each heaving breath and held her and said nothing, because really, what was there to say?

Other than *I missed you so much* and *take me back* and all the other stuff tough guys weren't supposed to say if they wanted to keep their pride.

But he didn't want his pride. He just wanted her. So he nearly said it. *Cara, I missed you every minute of every day.*

Maybe she knew it was coming because she sniffed and backed away. The only consolation was that she didn't actually shove him away the way she'd done the last time they parted. Six years ago when he'd come begging to her for a chance to explain.

A fly buzzed between them, and he waved it away.

"What's going on, Cara? What are you doing here?"

Her hands fluttered in the air until she took a deep breath and started in a quiet voice. "I work for TeleCel."

"The cell phone company? I thought you worked for that other one."

"TeleCel is a subsidiary, and I got an offer to come down here. To Panama."

Made sense; she was fluent in Spanish and a shooting star in her company. He knew, because yeah, he'd pumped his cousin Meredith for any news of Cara he could get. Meredith being friends with Cara's older sister meant he got news on a regular basis. But he hadn't heard about Panama.

"How long have you been here?"

"Just two months."

Two months. About the time he and his brother had been sailing in Belize on the boat they inherited from their grandfather. That was why he hadn't heard.

"Wait," she said abruptly. "How long have you been in Panama?"

"About three weeks."

They stared at each other in silence, and he swore she was thinking the same thought. *If only I'd known...*

Cara gave her head a little shake, and her long black locks rippled against each other. He had to take a deep breath before he could process anything else. Oh, talking. She was talking again.

"This part of Panama, from here to the Darien Gap, is the last big section of the Americas without cell phone coverage," she said. "Whoever gets a transmitter up Cerro Atrato first—" she pointed high, indicating some mountain peak "—will have conquered the last big chunk of virgin territory."

He glanced out at the simple huts of the village. A woman was beating a woven rug with a stick; a pig rooted near her feet.

"I don't get it. It's not like there are thousands of customers begging for cell phone coverage here."

She shook her head. "It would be a marketing coup more than a financial gain. TeleCel wants that. They need it. So they sent me here to get the chief to sign a deal. Just to helicopter in one little satellite dish. Nothing else. No chopping rain forest down, no intrusion. Just one transmitter."

"And what? These people are so pissed at the cell phone industry that they're holding you hostage?"

"No, they seemed okay with the deal. I'm sure it has to do with DigiOne."

"Digi who?"

"DigiOne, the only other major telecom provider down here. We're supposed to present to the investment group that put out the call for bids on this project on Friday. If DigiOne is the only company to present, we'll lose this deal."

He tried not to shrug. Who cared about some business deal?

She must have been reading his mind. "I'll lose my job, Tobin. The company brought me to Panama to win bids like this. I'll lose the reputation I've spent years building up. Do you know how hard it is to make it in this business?"

He knew how badly she craved success, yes. Something that hadn't made sense to him until he met her parents for the first time — a couple of hard-working immigrants who had their kids' high school diplomas framed on the living room wall. Their college diplomas, too — the ones they'd slaved away to pay for, because the daughters of the pizza parlor couple were going to end up much higher, much prouder than their humble roots. They had no choice. It was a matter of family pride.

Cara's parents had been thrilled when they found out she was bringing home the son of one of those blue-blooded American families. Like it was proof that the Leoni clan had made it in America. But they had counted on Tobin being someone more like his brother Seth — the good son who went to the right schools, got the right job, and got himself primed for the good life.

Tobin was the other brother, though. The one who got kicked out of the right schools. The one who got the wrong job, because what guy in his right mind used the Dartmouth degree he somehow managed to earn — because yes, in spite of everything, they'd let him in — to become a ski instructor? The way they saw it, Tobin achieved nothing better career-wise than a year-round tan. They didn't understand what an accomplishment it was to write his own script in a family like his.

But Cara did. She understood. Loved him for it. At least, he thought she had.

Then everything had come crashing down with a single misstep, and the one woman who'd made him think that he might someday get in step with the mainstream cut him off cold.

Cara's job was her life, her pride. Like hell, he would stand by and watch her lose it.

"So let's get you out of here."

She threw up her hands. "I can't. They won't let me. They're killing time until Friday, I'm sure of it."

He squinted at her. "When is this presentation?"

"Friday at three."

"So why isn't your company hauling ass to get you out of here?" If he were boss of that damn company, he'd have a whole search party out looking for Cara.

She scowled. "All I could get out was one quick message to a switchboard. And if Enrique gets it first—"

"Enrique?"

"My coworker who did the early legwork up here. He was furious when the company chose me to do the final negotiations instead of him."

"Furious enough to screw up this deal? To set you up?"

She tilted her head left then right. "I don't think he'd set me up, but he'd probably grab a golden opportunity if it came along. All he'd have to do is delete the message. Maybe pass on another one, like 'Cara called, and she'll be back soon.' Then when I don't show up for the meeting, I look like a fool. The company loses the bid, fires me, and presto — Enrique gets my job."

Tobin glanced through the narrow cut of a window to the tiny hamlet outside. "I don't get it. Why would this village keep you here? What do they care who gets the bid?"

She shrugged. "I'm guessing DigiOne has offered the village a better deal than TeleCel has."

"Can't you outbid them?"

"Not from here. I'm stuck. No phone. No ride."

She blinked at him and let five quiet seconds tick by.

He was about to say that she had him, and he had Lucy — clunky spark plugs and all — when a knock sounded at the door.

"*Señorita Leoni,*" came a voice.

"*Señora Leoni,*" he growled back. She was supposed to be his wife, right? Which made her a señora. "Come on, honey," he said, purring his best fake-husband voice in her ear. "Let's you and me go for a walk."

"A walk?"

He dropped his voice to conspiratorial level and winked. "A reconnaissance mission. Because I am here to bust you out of this joint."

Chapter Six

Cara opened the door on a very suspicious Rodrigo.

"*Senorita*— he started, but Tobin growled, so Rodrigo started again. "*Señora,* you didn't tell us you were expecting your husband."

Almost-husband, she wanted to say, and *I wasn't expecting him either.* She held her ground and tipped her chin up just a little bit, like her parents taught her. Pride. It was all a matter of pride. And sometimes, that meant covering up minor details like a racing heart and nerves that danced, just on seeing him again.

She strode out the door with Tobin in tow, trying to look like a woman who knew what she wanted.

Except she didn't. Everything had been clear until the moment Tobin showed up. She'd only wanted out of this village, pronto, and back to the office to pull together a first-class presentation that would knock the investors right out of their seats in their rush to award the bid to her. Well, to TeleCel. Then she could set her sights on the next project, and the next, and the next. Crawl into the bubble of work, work, and more work. Climb the ladder higher and higher. That was her mission in life.

Or it had been, until she'd met Tobin, all those years ago. He'd taught her a lot more than how to ski. He taught her how to live and love and laugh so hard, she shook. Taught her that time was worth more than money. That love could happen overnight and last a lifetime. That a woman who didn't need anyone might just need him.

"Why would she have to mention her husband?" Tobin cut in, hitting Rodrigo with a punch of a look. "If a man came here on a business trip, would you expect him to start talking about his wife?"

A thousand bonus points appeared on the scorecard her mind assigned to Tobin.

Rodrigo, who never looked anything but sly, suddenly looked apologetic. "No, no! I mean... What do you do, *Señor Leoni?*"

"I'm a photographer," Tobin answered, without bothering to correct the last name to his own. More bonus points.

"Where is your camera?"

She could feel Tobin stiffen beside her — couldn't miss it, because he had his arm around her shoulders, her body snug against his — but on the outside, he didn't miss a beat.

"I'm on vacation. My wife complains that I work too much." He said it with a chuckle, and she knew the inside joke. Working too much was probably the only thing he'd never been accused of by anyone. Not his parents, her parents, or any of the friends they'd once shared.

She frowned. Tobin was doing it again — bringing himself down by parroting their cutting remarks. But that wasn't fair. She'd seen him come home bone-tired and frozen after a twelve-hour day on the slopes. Seen him stick on a smile and say *sure* to the little kids who begged for just one more run with their favorite instructor. Seen him stay up long nights making last-minute changes to surf safari arrangements for whimsical clients. So what if his office was a mountainside or a beach? The man worked hard.

And played hard. That was the problem. Wherever Tobin went, a dozen adoring groupies went, too. All the weekends she spent polishing presentations and reports, he spent charming customers on the slopes. For all she knew, he'd been entertaining señoritas all the way down the coast.

Right on cue, a dozen critical voices piped up in her mind.

A guy like that is too popular for his own good. How could you ever trust him?

He'll never amount to anything. Why doesn't he get a real job?

She shook her head at herself. The past was the past. She had a job to do.

"And what are you doing for your vacation?" Rodrigo pressed on.

"I was thinking of staying here for a couple of days," Tobin said, and she nearly yelped. "Enjoy the rain forest. Visit the waterfall."

What did Tobin want with a waterfall? She needed to get out of here, now!

Rodrigo beamed. "Yes, you can stay. Visit the waterfall, interact with my people. Learn our ways. It's a fascinating culture. A small but important one."

"Do I get to wear a loincloth?"

Tobin was joking, but that didn't stop a little spike of heat from shooting through her body. Tobin in a loincloth... A little flap of fabric in front, two bare cheeks behind, round and tight. A sight for sore eyes.

Rodrigo launched into his favorite subject: finding a way to help his tribe move into the modern era while preserving traditional ways. In the short time she'd been in Panama, she'd heard a lot about indigenous groups and NGOs fighting for rights and representation, and Rodrigo seemed a true champion of the cause. A cause she could admire — except the part about keeping her hostage. She let her eyes drift over the village. How did they stand to benefit — or suffer — from TeleCel getting the antenna bid?

"*Señorita! Señorita!*" The kids came running up and towed her away to show her some kind of game with sticks and leaves. Amazing how creative kids without video games and TV could be.

She didn't notice that her right hand was still clasping Tobin's — tight — until the kids pulled her away. There was a little tug and she glanced back at him. His eyes held hers like a spotlight, as if the rain forest and village had faded away and it was just her. He had that crooked grin on that gave him a look halfway between star-struck and scheming.

Then the kids tugged again, and long after she slipped away, her fingers wiggled, wishing for his.

Chapter Seven

Tobin watched as a couple of girls came along and hooked Cara into what sounded like a word game of some kind. They'd point to something, say a word, and wait for her to repeat it so they could collapse into giggles, then point again. Their language was nothing like Spanish; it was full of hard sounds and guttural stops, and even Cara seemed to have trouble replicating the sounds. The best part was watching her giggle and laugh along. Watching her cock her head to listen, work her lips around the foreign syllables, and laugh again as the kids rolled in laughter all around her.

Cara. One of those people who was beautiful inside and outside. Any side, really.

Someone stole up to Tobin's elbow. Rodrigo. Again.

"Your wife, eh? I didn't see a ring."

Tobin rubbed a thumb against the finger where the engagement ring used to sit, a long time ago. "We left them at home. Didn't want something that precious stolen while we're traveling."

Rodrigo watched him like a snake. "Have you been married long?"

"Not long," Tobin whispered. "Not long at all." When he realized a couple of too-quiet seconds had ticked by and Rodrigo was still watching him, he cleared his throat roughly and turned his stare on Rodrigo, thinking thoughts like *Mine. Not leaving her. Ever.* He kept it up until Rodrigo dropped his eyes to the dirt and started digging with the tip of his bare toe.

That was more like it.

"You mess with my wife, man..." he growled, letting the threat trail off. It wasn't an act, either, except maybe for the *wife* part.

Rodrigo raised his hands quickly. "No one will harm her here, your wife."

Now, why did his chest go all warm when people called Cara his wife? Maybe because that was supposed to be the way it was. The way they belonged.

Except it hadn't quite worked out that way.

"Better not," Tobin shot back, though he'd already figured as much. But the village had some kind of hidden agenda, that was for sure.

He looked Rodrigo up and down. His wiry body and copper skin were just like those of the other villagers, but his perfect English and steel-rimmed glasses said this was a man who'd been out in the outside world.

The chief's nephew — wasn't that was Cara said? If anyone knew what was going on behind the scenes with the antenna deal, it would be Rodrigo.

"Rodrigo, have you been to the US?"

Rodrigo answered with a half smile that could have signaled pride or disgust. "Sure. Four years at UC Davis, two at Georgetown."

Now, why didn't that surprise him? "So you probably know the Eagles. The band."

"Sure."

"Then tell me, what's with the Hotel California thing you've got going on here?"

Rodrigo tried to hide his smile, but it was too big.

"Hotel California," Tobin pressed on. " 'You can check out any time you like, but you can never leave.' Sound familiar?"

The man wore his best poker face, but that didn't fool him.

"You don't want this antenna deal to happen?" Tobin prompted.

Rodrigo's eyes narrowed, like he was deciding how much to reveal.

"The antenna is coming," Rodrigo said at last. "The government has decided that." He scowled. "That is a battle I cannot win. But we can influence who wins the bid. The lesser of two evils."

Which meant DigiOne, Tobin figured. Cara's competition. "How much are they paying you to make her miss that meeting?"

Rodrigo stared a little longer then gave a little nod, like he'd decided no harm would come of the truth. "Enough for a new roof," he said quietly, pointing to an open-sided building. A couple of tiny voices trickled out of it, singing an alphabet song in Spanish for Cara. The makeshift village schoolhouse.

Shit.

Tobin eyed the crooked beams and the thatched roof, then kicked at the dirt. Leave it Cara to stumble across a rebel with a worthy cause. No wonder they were adamant that she stay.

"Tables and chairs, too. Right now, the children sit on the ground." Rodrigo's eyes were sparkling with vision now, so much that Tobin could see it, too: neat rows of desks and chairs with a dozen kids singing, laughing, learning. "And a world map on the wall," Rodrigo went on, "so they can be proud of where they come from but know what's outside. So they can choose, and choose wisely."

Tobin couldn't help but nod. Yeah, maybe he'd take a woman hostage, too, if it meant something like that to his hometown.

"I bet her company will match the deal, Rodrigo. Do better, even."

The man's face darkened. "Those men are old goats. They do not respect our ways. Do you know what they offered us? A new road. What do we need a new road for?"

Tobin could have tossed out a dozen good reasons. No more hiking in and out. No more mud. Quicker connections—

"We like it the way it is," Rodrigo said. "The bad road is like... our moat. It protects us from the outside world. From men who love money more than their souls — loggers, miners, smugglers. The drug runners are bad enough already." His eyes went dark as he shook his head. "No. Money for the school is much better than a road."

Probably Cara's company would be just as happy to fix the school as build a road or give the village anything else it wanted, but it was pretty clear they'd pissed Rodrigo off. His mind was made up. He'd do whatever necessary to make sure DigiOne won rights to the antenna. The village would get its school. Cara would lose her job. Tobin would... Wait, what did he have to win or lose?

The alphabet song hit a high note, and Cara's sweet voice carried above the rest.

He couldn't quite put it into words, but yeah, he had something on the line, too, even if he wasn't quite sure how much to hope. But he'd be damned if he'd give up his chance at... at whatever it was signaling madly in his gut. Not without a fight.

Chapter Eight

The sun set quickly in the tropics, but it still caught Tobin off guard. The beach town he'd spent the last couple of weeks in might be in the same small country, but Tucumba might as well have been a different planet. He was used to the whisper of waves over sand and an explosion of reds, oranges, and pinks on an open horizon. In the jungle, it was like God flipped a dimmer and let everything fade from sight.

Sights faded until all he could see was the lumpy outline of the rain forest canopy overhead. while his ears filled with a hum that grew in reverse proportion to the light. If the jungle was a bustling village by day, it was a partying city at night, with every living being in it contributing to the concert from every story of habitation. There were ear-level whistles, overhead hoots, scratches from underfoot. Tweets and scrapes he couldn't begin to trace, and the occasional low-toned growl that made even the locals huddle closer to their tiny fires.

Made Cara huddle closer to him, too, which made all kinds of body parts want to join the party, too. God, it had been too long. Too long without her.

A toothless old woman motioned them over to sit in the dirt across from each other, separated by a fallen log, then made them stretch out their forearms. She took out a hollowed-out gourd filled with something and started scratching it into his skin, using a stick like a pencil.

"Ouch!" He tried pulling his arm back, but the woman was surprisingly strong.

Cara just giggled. "It's jagua. A fruit extract. It keeps the mosquitoes away."

"Does it work?" He grimaced as the woman etched a complicated pattern of black lines into his skin.

"I guess we'll see." The way Cara said it hinted at something else.

He looked up and found her eyes and stayed there a long, long time while the rest of the world — the screeching jungle, the scratching on his skin, the chicken muttering by his foot — all faded away. Far away, until it was just him and his princess and a whole lot of pheromones filling the air. The kind that let his imagination take them right back to their hut.

Just when it seemed Cara was letting her guard down, he sensed her tense back up. He followed her frosty gaze across the clearing to a man who had just stepped into sight.

"Who's that?"

She rolled her eyes. "Jean-Philippe Lefebvre. Some anthropologist type. Not too keen on outsiders."

That was pretty clear from the way the man stomped over like a charging bull. Wiry and tall, he seemed even taller once he got close. Tobin fought the urge to jump to his feet and let his height do the talking. Instead, he shot out a casual, *"Hola."*

"Who are you?" the man demanded, staring him down through bloodshot eyes. "What do you want here?"

Cara, he nearly said, but swallowed it down. Not the point right now. "Tobin Cooper. Pleased to meet you."

The man looked at him in disgust. God, what an asshole.

From a distance, the man could pass as a local, but up close, a foreign accent and gray-brown hair gave him away. The scent of dope hung over his wiry frame and his heavily lined face.

"Let me guess," Tobin continued. "You're French."

"Belgian," the man all but spit back. "And you? American?" He said it like a curse.

"Yup. Nice to meet you, Jean-Claude."

The man's glare went to death mode. "Jean-Philippe."

Whatever.

The man huffed and stomped off, and even the old woman painting Tobin's arms rolled her eyes.

"What's his problem?"

"Me. You. Us." Cara shrugged. "He barely talks to me. Like I don't exist."

Moron. What kind of man would ignore a woman like Cara?

"He's some kind of expert on indigenous languages and cultures," Cara went on.

An expert on hallucinogens of the jungle would have been Tobin's guess, but he kept his mouth shut.

"Apparently, he's written a book."

Tobin shrugged. "Any idiot can write a book."

"Lefebvre seems to treat the village like his own private turf. Like any outsider is a threat to his little fiefdom."

"Seems to me he's been playing Tarzan a little too long."

"And mixing a little too much of the local weed with his chicha," Cara added, shaking her head. "But whatever. Live and let live."

Tobin watched Lefebvre trot up to Rodrigo. The angry gestures he made in their direction hardly suggested *live and let live*. More like *kick the hell out*.

But, of course, Rodrigo didn't want to let Cara out. And from the looks of it, Rodrigo won, because Lefebvre turned from him and stomped away.

Apparently, even tiny jungle villages had their share of rivalries and intrigues. It might have given him a good laugh if Cara wasn't stuck in the middle.

The old woman finished painting his arms with a satisfied sound and shooed them over to an open-sided hut. They sat on a log by a tiny spit of a fire, eating dinner while a dozen little kids looked on like this was their favorite television sitcom — the one with the funny gringa who didn't know how to eat with her hands. He had a leg up on Cara in that department, for sure.

Lefebvre scowled from the shadows, sitting apart from the rest, while Rodrigo and an old man who had to be the local chief ate quietly across the way.

Lefebvre, he wasn't sure about, but the villagers didn't mean Cara any harm. For one thing, he believed Rodrigo. For another, the villagers' smiles were too genuine, their patient nods too indulging. They seemed delighted to share what they had, piling not only Cara's plate but his too with a big meal — of what, he couldn't quite tell. Rice and a side of meat that was tough and gamey.

"Tastes like chicken," he announced to no one in particular.

"Yes, but is it?" Cara whispered.

"Do you really want to know?" He'd seen some kids catch frogs earlier and spotted a snake carcass — a big one — hanging by a shed.

Cara shook her head.

"You been eating like this all week?"

"Yeah," she sighed and rapped her knuckles against the log. "Knock on wood, I haven't gotten sick. Yet." Then she jutted her chin toward the tiny old woman stirring the rice pot. "But they've been really nice. Feeding me, showing me how they make baskets, everything. The only thing they don't let me do is leave."

"Ah, but tomorrow is another day."

He didn't have to look to know she was shooting him a suspicious look. "Tobin, what are you doing here?"

The same question he was asking himself. What was he doing here, other than getting a hard-on just from sitting next to his Italian princess? Was he going to bust her out of this joint or not? A couple more days stuck in the rain forest didn't suit her, but it sure suited him. Sunday — the day they'd let her go — was four days away, and four days with Cara was more than he ever thought he'd get a chance at. Four days to imprint every part of her on his mind forever. Her scent. Her voice. Her laugh, if he could coax it out of her again. Four days spent filling his tanks with every impression he could stuff in his memory before she marched out of his life once and for all.

Tempting. Very tempting.

Except that wouldn't be right, and he knew it. Better to stick to the plan. Get Cara out. Maybe get a little bit of closure. Then he could finish out the next month on the beach, head home and...do what?

Cara, as usual, seemed to be reading his mind. "So, what are you doing in Panama, anyway?"

Other than rescuing her and surfing some fairly sweet breaks? But that wasn't what she was asking, and he knew it.

"My granddad died last winter," he started, then stopped when Cara put a hand on his and turned those coal-black eyes on him, wide and sincere.

"Oh, Tobin. He was so sweet."

His heart tightened just a little, like it always did when he thought of the only person who'd ever really believed in him. "Yeah, he was the best."

And for a minute, the two of them sat there quietly.

"He left us his boat," Tobin started again.

Cara's eyes went wider, and he just about drowned looking in them. *"Serendipity?"* She said it in a reverent whisper.

"Yeah, *Serendipity.* He left it in his will, saying he wanted us — all of his grandkids — to get out on it for a while. Remember what's important. Family. Memories. All that." He finished quickly, waving a hand in the air in case it came across as too sentimental. "So Seth and I sailed down here—"

"You and your brother sailed that little boat all the way from Boston to the Caribbean?" Her jaw went slack.

He added that to his memory bank. How good it felt to impress someone. Well, to impress Cara.

"Yeah. And you know what? Three months on a thirty-two-foot boat together and we managed not to kill each other, or hit a reef, or get lost." *Or shot or arrested,* part of his mind added, though they'd come pretty close. "It was actually a good time." *A really good time,* he nearly said. Just him and his brother, getting to know each other all over again.

"Wow. Where is Seth now? Where's the boat?"

He grinned just thinking about it. "Seth's never been better. He's still on the boat, with his girlfriend, Julie."

Her eyebrows shot up. "Seth found time for something other than his job?"

Tobin shot her a look that said, *There's the pot calling the kettle black.*

She ignored it. "How serious a girlfriend?"

"Well, he looks at her like he's the Earth and she's the sun." He got stuck there, because that's how it had been with him and Cara. Christ, that's how it still was, even though she'd shoved him all the way out by Pluto.

Still, on a night like this, with a fire crackling and the crickets chirping, he could just about pretend everything was okay again.

He swallowed a little and went on. "Julie's great. She's dragged out the pirate side of him."

Cara laughed. "Seth has a pirate side?"

If only she knew some of their escapades in Belize. If only he had time to tell her some of the stories she'd missed. Too bad six years made for a hell of a lot of stories, and they only had a couple of days.

He swallowed the last bit of rice and pretended that was what had him gulping so hard.

"You ought to see the guy. Barefoot, no watch, no cell phone. They're sailing to Bonaire right now. Bringing the boat to Meredith and Mia. It's their turn next."

"Everyone gets a turn on the boat?"

"Yep. Every set of siblings. That's what Gramps wanted; that's what we'll do."

"Cool," she whispered, staring into the flames.

He stared, too, and between the licks of fire he saw an image of *Serendipity*, cutting through the waves. With Cara at the wheel and him working the lines, the two of them sailing into a future together.

He squeezed his lips together. Yeah, well, at least his brother got his happy ending.

Chapter Nine

If being stuck in the village for five days had been a trial of patience, being stuck in a honeymoon-sized bungalow with Tobin for five minutes was a trial of virtue. Especially after that cryptic comment he made when Rodrigo asked what sight-seeing he wanted to do the next day.

Sightseeing? She could have screamed.

But Tobin only grinned. "I'm not sure." He had his arm around her like she really was his wife, and he chose exactly that moment to squeeze her closer and shoot Rodrigo one of those man-to-man winks. "We'll have to sleep on it tonight."

We'll?

And there he was, two steps away from her in the confines of the tiny cabin, looking at her like *that*. Like he used to on nights when going to bed didn't mean they were going to sleep.

It was hell. The sizzling, sinful side of hell. Because Tobin seemed to take out every weapon in his arsenal and spit-polish it in full view. The winning smile that put a dimple in his left cheek. The rumbling baritone, the accidental brush-ups that had her body on fire. The man was temptation in jungle camo.

And then he started to strip.

"Hey!" she yelped. "What are you doing?"

His eyes sparkled as he looked up from unbuttoning his fly. "What?" His voice was pure innocence wrapped around sheer seduction. "I always sleep in the buff. You know that."

God, did he have to do that sexy eyebrow thing?

"But this is different," she insisted, telling her nipples to sit down.

"Different how?" He slid his khaki pants down and made a show of working them around his ankles. That left just the mouth-watering sight of him in blue boxers. Boxers that housed a nice, tight bundle. His thumbs hooked in the waistband.

She shot him a killer look. *You wouldn't.*

His eyes laughed and said, *Watch this.*

And he did, and she did, and when he got the boxers all the way off, he sauntered over to the old-fashioned washstand in the corner of the room and stood there, buck naked, brushing his teeth.

He still had that perfect ass, that perfect taper of the waist that shot out to his broad chest. Chiseled shoulders, muscled back. He was watching her when she remembered to yank her eyes back up to his.

Caught ogling. Damn. But how she could help it? Even with a toothbrush in his mouth, he looked like a million bucks. If she had her camera, the pictures could have set off an advertising campaign for just about any product. Toothpaste. Aftershave. Upmarket four-wheel drives. Women would flock in droves to buy whatever it was he was selling. Men, too, if just in hopes that a little of Tobin's magic might jump over to them. Because it wasn't just his looks. It was the sparkle, the vivacity that did it.

And at that moment, he wasn't selling anything at all. Just good old Tobin, smiling away.

Buck naked.

He turned and motioned to her with the toothbrush. "You wanna use it?"

It was reminiscent of their first morning together, in too many ways. Too many memories. Good ones. Hot ones. Soft ones, too, like him tracing a finger over her eyebrow, looking at her like he'd scored some kind of goddess of the night instead of plain old Cara.

"Sure," she squeaked, fighting to keep her eyes on his face.

His arm brushed her shoulder as he stepped past.

Her heart rate jumped high and stayed high. Her eyes stuck to the mirror, watching him lift the mosquito netting and slide into bed. A double bed that would fit one person well and two people cozily. Didn't bother to throw the sheet over himself, either — he just lay there, hands behind his head, cock jutting toward his right hip in the early warm-up stage of arousal.

She stalled and stalled, but the mosquitoes eventually won out. She dropped her shorts but not her panties, pulled her bra off under her shirt, and crawled under the netting. In bed. With Tobin.

Jesus Christ.

He spoke before she could start her speech about his side, her side, and the no-go zone in between.

"So, you ever been married before?"

She thumped him on the arm. "Tobin! We are not married!"

"We are for now," he said, and she could hear the grin in his voice. "I kind of like it."

"Purely a business arrangement." God, she sounded snippy.

There was a long silence in which she couldn't tell if he was angry, disappointed, or amused. She didn't dare look, although her body had all its feelers out for other cues.

"Right, business," he murmured at last.

There used to be a time when she could see past the screen he put up in front of his soul. Tonight, though, he was a stranger.

To her mind, at least. Her body was yearning to slide into its favorite spot, with her chin between the flat plates of his pecs and one leg looped over his thigh. The way she'd drifted off to sleep on a thousand happy nights, once upon a time.

She sighed, and it came out much too loudly for that small a space.

"Tired?"

"Exhausted," she lied. She wouldn't get a wink of sleep lying next to him.

"Then sweet dreams," he whispered, low and sultry. "I know I'll be having some."

"Turn off the light already. And stay on your side. I mean it."

The sheets rustled in a quiet tease. "No goodnight kiss?"

Definitely not. "Goodnight."

"Goodnight, *mi marida*."

She almost corrected him. *Goodnight, mi mujer.* My wife. But she caught herself just in time. She wasn't his wife, and he wasn't her husband.

She lay there, listening to the mosquitoes searching for a breach in the netting. Listening to his breathing. Sniffing his masculine scent. Wishing he'd come sneaking over the demarcation line and let the kindling crackling inside her ignite.

Minutes stretched. Yawned. Trudged painfully on their way to nothingness until Tobin huffed, punched his pillow, and flicked the flashlight on.

She sat up, pulling the sheet up to her chin. "What are you doing?"

He moved the light over a patch of wall. "Sweetheart, I can jack off two inches away from your luscious hip, or I can try to distract myself. You prefer that I jack off?" His voice rose in hope.

"I prefer that you don't," she managed, even though the image appealed to the cavewoman in her. Images like wrapping her hand over his and helping him work the tension off. Like sliding into a straddle over his waist and—

"You offering to help?" His voice was low and growly.

"Certainly not."

"Didn't think so." He sighed. "So, distraction. Here's the game. See the wall over there?" The flashlight threw a diffuse spotlight through the curtain-like net.

"Um, yes?"

"See the gecko?" He pointed with the flashlight, and yes, there it was, a gecko stuck motionless to the wall with his suction-cup feet. Kind of cute, but their scurrying steps had kept her up most of the past nights.

She nodded, wishing he'd turn the flashlight on himself instead. Like on those abs of his. She could check out the box pattern there, invent her own game...

Heartless man that he was, he clicked the light off and started counting. "One, two, three..." His fingers tapped on the sheet. "...nine...ten. Okay, time to guess which direction the gecko moved to. North, south, west, or east?"

"Uh, south?"

He clicked the light on, and there was the gecko, two steps east of where he'd been a moment before.

"My point," Tobin said.

Only a man could make a competition out of watching reptiles. But hey, she was game, especially if it took her mind off his abs. And other parts. "Again."

He clicked the light off and counted from one to ten. "Your guess?"

"North," she said and cheered a second later when the light came on. "My point!"

"A tie, then." He turned the light off, and this time, she did the counting.

Two clicks later, Tobin was two points ahead and chuckling. "You know what happens when I get three points ahead?"

"Game over?"

"Not until I get my prize."

"Prize?" Her gut tightened and her heart went pitter-pat.

"A kiss," he whispered. The word hung in the air as he clicked the light off.

The obvious reply was to huff, turn toward the opposite wall, and end this stupid game. So what did her impulsive Italian heart make her do?

"One..." She started counting, and it was a challenge. "Two..."

"Three." There was a smile in his voice. "Four..."

Her heart thumped through the ten beats, then two more. He was torturing her.

"Guess," he prompted.

So far, the gecko had progressed north twice, east once, and west once, but never south.

"South," the vixen in her blurted before the good girl could protest.

He chuckled and clicked the light on. "North. You owe me a kiss."

Part of her was doing a crazy victory dance, the other part groaning. What had she been thinking?

"Come on, fair's fair." He turned to her and puckered up.

"Tobin! I am not kissing those lips! You look like a cartoon character."

He broke into a smile so wide, so like the old times when they'd had fun and played and talked and didn't worry about things like trust because it never occurred to them that there was anything else, that something in her clicked and she leaned over to deliver his prize.

She had a split-second view of his grin fading to surprise, and then there was only the kiss. The silk of his lips and the light touch of his hand closing over her back. The warmth of him, the taste of something so good, she needed more.

His mouth fit exactly over hers, and the taste was of a place where the mountains meet the sea. She slid her tongue along his lips, then dipped inside, and everything in her soared. His hand slid along her waist, and she nestled closer, driven by a rising wave of need. It was like they'd never left off. Like everything a soul needed for well-being was in that kiss. Warmth and honesty and a nurturing touch that—

Something on the rooftop fluttered and chirped, and Cara pulled back with a sharp inhale. Jesus, was that her, giving him mouth-to-mouth?

It was. And she wanted more. Lots more. Now.

But there were six long years between that kiss and the one that came before it, and all of a sudden she got cold feet.

His eyes flashed and his lips quirked, but he didn't say anything. Just cupped her ribs in his big hands and waited.

"Tobin, we need to talk."

The corners of his eyes drooped. "We've talked enough."

"I mean, about back then. About what happened."

And poof, the little magic bubble that had formed around them popped. The rain forest was back, and all its citizens were shaking their heads in disappointment.

She wanted to reel back the words and say something else — better yet, do something else, like fall into another kiss, but it was too late. The silence that ticked by took forever doing so, stretching and pulling until she wanted to hide under the sheet.

When Tobin spoke again, his voice was low and gravelly. "I did not touch that woman that night."

Chapter Ten

"I know," she whispered.

"You know?"

She nodded to the ceiling because she still couldn't meet his eyes. "Your brother and Meredith told me."

The quieter he got, the louder her heart thumped.

"They told you." He said it with a scary lack of intonation.

She nodded, remembering that awful feeling when they had. That feeling of every drop of hope draining out of her. Appalled at how quickly she'd jumped to the wrong conclusion.

"They told you the only reason I left that stupid stag party with that girl was to get her home safely," he went on.

Every muscle in her body was stiff, and she barely dipped her chin. "They said that two drunk guys were getting ready to take that woman who knows where. That she was drunk, too, and barely conscious. If you hadn't stepped in, anything could have happened."

The air moved between them as he shook his head. "That girl was barely over drinking age, if she cleared it at all."

If only she'd gotten the full story right away. But all she heard was that Tobin had taken a drunk girl to her place and disappeared inside.

"The minute I got her to her place, she threw up," he muttered. "You know how long it took to clean myself up? To clean her up enough that she wouldn't choke on it?"

Long enough to make it look like something else entirely. She closed her eyes at the familiar wave of shame. God, if only she hadn't jumped to her own conclusion, like everyone else.

"That's all I did." He didn't have a hand over his heart, but he didn't need one. The crack in his voice was promise enough.

"I know," she said, but it barely came out above the chorus of crickets outside.

It had taken Meredith and Seth a week to track down the girl, her roommate, and the neighbor, and another two weeks to set the story straight. Every day of it, an eternity of tears and pain, then shame.

Tobin rolled to face her, his head propped on a hand, his elbow on the mattress, so she couldn't avoid his eyes. "If you know I didn't do it, why are you still mad at me?"

She wanted to jump up and insist she wasn't mad, but she was. Mad at him for letting her go so easily. Mad at herself for being stupid enough to believe he would ever hurt her. A mistake that ruined everything, and even though it wasn't his fault, he was the one who came away tarnished. No, he hadn't cheated, people whispered, but one day he probably would. A man not to be trusted, a party boy.

By the time she got the real story, Tobin was gone. Far gone — on a surf trip to Australia where the rumormongers had him shacked up with a different surfer girl every night. A man that good-looking wouldn't be lonely for long. Not on a ski slope, not on a beach, not on the other side of the world.

Every muscle in her body wanted to follow him and haul him home, but she'd stopped just short of booking a flight.

Where's your pride, girl? Her sister's words had been a slap in the face.

Damn pride. That and an awful, gnawing doubt. Even if he hadn't cheated on her this time, one day, he just might. Life was a game to Tobin; why wouldn't he want to play around?

You can't trust a man like him, her mother said.

Why can't you find someone like his brother? her dad had thrown in.

Her eyes stung and salty and she lay stiff as a log, trying to hold it all in.

She didn't want his brother. She didn't want any of the dull, straitlaced men she'd tried dating over the years. She wanted him.

Still wanted him, deep down in her heart.

"Maybe it was a good thing." Tobin shrugged, settling onto his back again. He tried to make it sound light, but she could hear the defeat in his words. "If you were ready to believe I'd be interested in anyone else, then maybe we weren't ready to get married."

God, the truth hurt.

"Your dad was right," he added, and when she looked, she saw that the face that wasn't capable of anything but joy was suddenly lined with sorrow.

Her dad called him a no-good bum and a lot of other things right before he started throwing chairs to chase Tobin away.

Tobin, who'd never let her down. Who never would have.

And here was the proof. Of all the people in the world to come to her rescue, it was Tobin here in the jungle, promising to find a way out.

He rolled away, and all she could see was the hard wall of his back. When he spoke, it was in a choked whisper.

"Good night, Cara."

Chapter Eleven

Cara didn't sleep a wink. The previous nights, the unfamiliar jungle noise had kept her up, but now it was worse, as if each of the rain-forest dwellers had taken on one of her emotions. The haunting hoots of an owl echoed her regrets. The resonating song of the cricket amplified her shame. And the sweet calls of songbirds embodied everything she could have had, but lost.

Tobin was awfully quiet on his side of the bed, but leave it to the big lug, he started the next morning fresh and chipper and sunny as ever. He stretched and smiled and ducked under the mosquito net to splash water on his face.

"Morning," he called, as if he knew it was going to be the world's greatest day. The man always woke up like that. "Gotta pee!"

Always ready with a smile and a funny line. That was Tobin.

He pulled on his shorts and headed out the door, where he was immediately intercepted by a host of giggling children.

"Morning!" he said. "*Buenos días*, to you, and you, and you."

His fan club erupted into happy sounds. Typical Tobin, spreading the gospel of simple joy and happiness wherever he went.

Maybe she could learn a little from him.

Cara stretched out under the sheet, contemplating the thatched roof. Then she frowned. What was that, pressing on her leg?

She lifted her head to check... and nearly passed out.

Two beady eyes watched her closely, and a forked tongue darted out.

Every muscle in her body twitched, fighting the instinct to flee.

The head was flat and evil, the eyes black. Glittering scales on a body as thick as her arm. A diamond pattern rippled and blurred as she focused on the eyes. *Oh my God. Oh my God, oh my God. . .*

The snake lifted its head, clearly thinking more along the lines of *Lunch, lunch, lunch.*

If she flung the sheet over its head, would it still bite? Would the venom go through the bedding? Would she die a horribly slow and painful death?

A shadow darkened the doorway, and Tobin pranced back in. "Rise and shine, princess." He went to the washbasin and started brushing his teeth.

Tobin! she screamed wildly inside.

He started humming "Bare Necessities" from *The Jungle Book.*

Tobin! Her lips formed his name, but no sound came out. It was just like being a kid, when she'd imagined monsters in the shadows and called out for her mom — quietly, so the monsters couldn't hear.

But that snake was no trick of her imagination. She'd seen enough pictures in her guide books to recognize one of the most venomous snakes in the Americas: a fer-de-lance.

"Tobin!" A tiny croak came out, and the snake advanced with a sickening ripple of yellow scales over her leg. The head hovered over her hip, and its eyes never left her face.

Call him, those eyes dared her. *Call him and I will bite.*

"How did you slee—" Tobin turned and froze. "Whoa."

Whoa was right. She was staring death in the face.

Tobin stabbed the air with his toothbrush. "I'll be right back."

He dashed out the door, and she could have wailed, *Don't leave me! Not now!*

Not ever! another part of her wailed.

Tobin rooted around outside, rustling and swearing, but all she saw were the two tiny nose slits and two reptilian eyes.

"Okay." Tobin loomed in the doorway with something long and silvery in his hand. A machete? He was going to hack the snake to death — on her body?

"Tobin!" she squeaked.

He flicked his wrist, turning the blade this way and that, trying to figure out an angle that would work. "Um...okay, so..."

"Tobin!" she shrieked.

And just like that, Tobin went from indecision to pure action. His body blurred, metal flashed, and the cool, flat slide of steel slid along her leg. Tobin flung the snake backward and pounced, machete raised. He brought it crashing down to the cabin floor, out of her sight, and there was a dull thunk. The blade came up bloody before crashing back down. *Thunk! Thunk!* By which point she was screaming and out of the bed and behind Tobin, jumping from leg to leg as if the floor were crawling with scorpions. And who knew? Maybe those were next.

Tobin stood in front of her, armed and mighty and practically baring his teeth. A minute ticked by before he pointed with the machete.

"Breakfast, anyone?"

His voice was joking, but the hug he caught her in a second later was serious. Dead serious.

"Jesus," she whispered, closing her eyes to the mess. "I have to get out of this place."

A broad hand stroked her hair, and his lips flitted over her forehead. The man was steel and cotton at the same time, all hard plates of muscle with a soft, soothing touch.

"I'll get you out of here, Cara. I swear I will."

And for the first time in days — maybe even years, it felt like somehow, everything might just turn out all right.

She waited for the funny comment Tobin was sure to make. The tease. Something about snakes and bites and sex, maybe. Or something about princesses stuck in the jungle, followed by a flash of his perfect teeth and knee-melting smile.

But he didn't. He looked at her long and hard, as if a whole speech was perched on the tip of his tongue, dying for him to work up the courage to set it free.

The words never came, though. He closed his eyes briefly, let her get dressed then quietly shooed her out the door.

Maybe it wasn't the same old Tobin as before. This one was a little older, a little wiser. A little quieter, too.

He came out silently, the snake looped over his machete.

His machete.

Holy shit.

He tossed the carcass in the bushes then came back to her side.

"See?" He kicked aside leaves, clearing a trail. "The coast is clear."

The man was a prince.

No one in the village seemed to bat an eye at the sight of the snake. One man, though, sat on a tree stump across the clearing, watching them closely. Lefebvre. Looking like he'd been waiting for them to come out — or waiting for them to never come out. Was that a scowl of disappointment or just his usual disdain?

"*Señora! Señor!*" A woman beckoned them over for breakfast. It had been like that every morning: with no ado whatsoever, someone would smile and wave and offer a plate. In fact, there were often a couple of people vying for the honor of feeding her.

But breakfast, at a time like this?

Tobin, of course, dug right in.

Cara gave the ground a good stomp to chase away any lurking snakes before sitting down and accepting a plate of fried plantains.

"You think if a couple of these people showed up in your hometown, anyone would spontaneously offer them a warm meal?" Tobin mused between munches.

She snorted. The villagers had taught her a lot of things besides basket-weaving and which plants — and snakes — to avoid. Things like generosity, openheartedness, neighborliness.

On the other hand, they were keeping her captive, too.

She shook her head, not knowing what to believe. "For all we know, they could have slipped the snake into our cabin."

"Nah," Tobin countered, shoveling another plantain into his mouth. Totally relaxed, like he started every day by killing venomous snakes and eating with his bare hands. "I think it came in through the roof."

Like that made her feel better.

"That, or he did it." Tobin's voice dropped and his eyes narrowed on Lefebvre, who glared back.

Cara didn't want to believe the anthropologist would go that far, but still...

Tobin kicked the ground then stuck a smile back on.

"Delicious!" he announced, and all the ladies clucked in approval.

Rodrigo showed up halfway through Tobin's third helping, wearing a green T-shirt with a picture of a bulldozer circled and crossed out by a red line. "I will organize a guide, so you can see the waterfall."

Cara wanted to moan. The last thing she wanted was a jungle hike. She wanted out, now more than ever.

"Great!" Tobin said. "I can't wait to see the birds."

"You like birds?" Rodrigo looked delighted.

Cara crooked an eyebrow. Since when did Tobin like birds?

"Sure, I'm an amateur orni—" Either he got stuck on the word, or he was having fun. "A horny...an ormi—"

She lifted her eyebrows. "An ornithologist?"

He stuck another banana in his mouth and pointed at her with a look that said, *Bingo!*

Rodrigo pointed uphill, but Tobin shook his head.

"Not the top of the waterfall." He pointed down, in the direction of the valley with the bridge. The way out. "The bottom." He said it so casually, she knew something was up.

Rodrigo eyed Tobin the way one might study a sleeping anaconda. "Why the bottom?"

Yes, she wanted to echo, *why the bottom?*

"I saw a waterfall in Honduras that people say is the most beautiful in all Central America, but when I saw the one here yesterday, I thought it might be a contender. But I'd need to see from the bottom to be sure."

Rodrigo looked positively outraged. "Our waterfall is the most beautiful. People come from all over the world to see it."

"That's why I want to go. To see for myself. From the bottom."

What was this obsession with the bottom of the falls?

"It's very far," Rodrigo warned.

"I love hiking," Tobin countered.

Since when?

"And I love butterflies."

"I thought you said you liked birds."

She could see his mind racing. "I like birds. But butterflies are my passion." The man even managed to say it with a straight face. "And they're most active around now, so we need to get going."

Tobin liked butterflies about as much as he liked the opera music her father listened to.

"It's much closer to visit the top," Rodrigo warned.

"How close?"

"Only about an hour."

Tobin nodded. "That'll be on our list for tomorrow. Today we want the view from the bottom."

"The bottom," Rodrigo repeated. He scrutinized Tobin's poker face.

"The bottom is the best place to appreciate the height of a waterfall. But whatever." Tobin flapped his hand, as if was all the same to him. "I'm pretty sure that waterfall in Honduras is nicer, anyway."

Rodrigo muttered under his breath and stalked away in search of a guide.

She sidled up to Tobin. "A hike? And another one tomorrow?"

He nodded, looking ridiculously pleased with himself.

"Tomorrow is Friday," she went on. "And the presentation is at three. I need to get out of this place. I thought you came to save me."

Tobin inched closer. Closer. Kissing close. Not a good thing, because a happy, confident Tobin did deadly things to her resolve. Just like the day she met him on the ski slope: the minute she saw him, she went hot all over. And not just because of his looks. It was more than that, like her soul already knew he was the only man for her. She'd fought the attraction all day, only to end up in bed with him that very same night. And loved every minute of it.

She blinked a few times, because thinking about hot nights with Tobin was not doing anything for her cause.

"Where's your sense of adventure?"

When he grinned at her like that, she could have swung Tarzan-style through the trees to get to him. Wrap her legs around him. Dive into his mouth with her tongue.

"Tobin, why are really you here?"

He leaned in so close, she thought he might kiss her. "I came because I heard you were in trouble."

She could feel his soft breath on her cheek, smell that uniquely Tobin scent that always reminded her of schnapps: fruity but hard-hitting. The kind of scent that didn't come in a bottle, only on him.

"I am in trouble."

"I mean, like big trouble. Mortal danger. Damsel in distress." He flashed a winning smile, and she nearly bought it. That smile was Tobin's weapon and his weakness, because most people couldn't see past the sheer voltage of it to the soul beneath.

But she saw, and it made her heart skip. He was serious behind the smile. Dead serious. Worried — for her. His eyes said he would have fought his way into a guerrilla camp for her. Parachuted onto an erupting volcano. Those eyes promised he'd never, ever let anything happen to her. He'd keep her safe.

From anything but her own stupidity.

Her chin started to dip in shame, but he tilted it back up with one finger. "Look, I will get you out of here. Soon. But for now, we make like we're here to enjoy life in the slow lane. So we'll play with the kids, visit the waterfall. Smell the roses, or whatever kind of flowers those giant yellow things are." He motioned overhead. "And all the time, we're looking for a way to get out."

She glanced in Lefebvre's direction and hid a shiver.

"But how? Every time I get more than one hundred yards, they herd me back in. Always polite, never with force," she added, because his gaze narrowed like he might just let his hidden dragon out. "But no matter what I try, I'm stuck."

He reached out to tuck a strand of hair behind her ear, and he left his fingers there much longer than necessary. Then he twitched a little and went from sad to sneaky with a mischievous wink. "I think the waterfall is a great place to start bird-watching, don't you think?"

Chapter Twelve

Off they went, through the thick of the rain forest with three local men, each of them carrying a blowgun and a bundle of darts. *Guides*, Rodrigo called them. His code word for *guards*.

"Are those things really tipped with poison?" Tobin muttered out of the side of his mouth.

She nodded. "I've seen them make it. Serious stuff. They hunker down and do it carefully. Keep the kids out of arm's reach. I've seen it work, too."

"Yeah, so have I — in one of those TV documentaries my parents made me watch." He grinned. "Kind of cool to see them for real, as long as they're not pointed my way."

One of the men stopped, crouched, and aimed his blowgun into the foliage. There was a *thwooo-whack!* and a flutter in the foliage as his prey fell. One of the boys scampered off trail and came back with a bird. Stone dead.

"Yeah, I guess now's not the time to make a break for it," Tobin murmured.

She shook her head. Even if they could evade the darts, they'd never get across the bridge with its machine gun-toting guards. They'd had a glimpse from a cliff's edge, but only a hint before the trail wound farther east, downriver and away from the bridge.

No. Escape was not on the menu for today. Would it ever be?

She resigned herself to the walk and whatever secret plan Tobin was scheming at.

Even with Friday itching at the back of her mind, though, Cara found herself a bit too distracted to think clearly of escape as the walk stretched on. Distracted by Tobin. That her mountain god of a ski instructor could morph into a beach hunk and offer surf lessons straight from a woman's fantasies, she already knew. But now he had the Indiana Jones look down pat, too. Him and his swinging machete and the bag slung across his shoulders and the shirt sticking to his back, showing every ripple of muscle.

A good thing the jungle dwellers were in full song; that covered up the throaty sigh she let out. Everything from blue-and-yellow tree frogs to rainbow-colored macaws to camouflaged insects croaked, whistled, and sang in full voice all around them, filling eight stories of rain forest with gossip. A howler monkey growled like a lion, and a sloth hung upside down from a branch.

"Now that's my kind of guy," Tobin quipped.

Stop it! She wanted to yell. *Stop begging people to think that's you!*

Tobin ambled on, head turning every which way like he didn't want to miss a square inch. Like he was *enjoying* being a captive of the world's most hospitable hostage-takers. Her inner lens snapped and clicked as her mind scribbled a caption to go with it. *A man who knows how to live.*

She followed his gaze left, right, up, and down. The rain forest was dangerous, but gorgeous, too — not just in its grandest elements, but in the microscopic details. Tree roots thicker than her waist rose eight feet off the ground and formed intricate lace patterns. Miniature highways packed with a rush hour of ants bisected the trail, paying the human intruders no mind. The jungle pulsed with life, like the heartbeat of the earth. Tobin wasn't swinging the machete for show, either; the forest grew so fast, each day threw another dozen vines across the winding mud trail.

With every stroke of the silver blade, the fabric of his shirt shifted and stretched. She frowned, recognizing it. Why did Tobin still insist on wearing that stupid shirt?

Waynston Prep, said the scrolling script. Underneath was a fancy crest and a date: *1832.* Worn, torn, and stained, that shirt was everything a fancy prep school shirt shouldn't be.

"Waynston Prep!" Her mom had practically clapped when she'd first met Tobin. "A great school. You went there?"

"I did." He'd flashed a charming grin, then shattered the effect. "Until they threw me out."

Cara remembered it perfectly: how her parents had exchanged horrified glances. How she kept straining for him to explain what really happened. But he didn't. He just smiled and chowed down on the lasagna and told her mother how delicious dinner was.

That was the thing. Tobin never bothered to explain. She'd only managed to drag the story out of his brother bit by bit. For all the pranks Tobin had played in school, he'd only been expelled when he claimed responsibility for bringing alcohol into the dorms. All to save the skin of his roommate, the inner-city kid on scholarship who'd get no second chances in life.

She'd glared at Tobin that night, urging him to finish the story. *Explain it, Tobin. Explain.*

But Tobin just shot her a bittersweet look. *They'll never believe me anyway.*

That was Tobin: principled to a fault, even when he had to pay a heavy price. Resigned to his fate. Did he wear the shirt as a reminder of failure or of doing the right thing?

She hung her head. High school wasn't the only time he'd done the right thing, nor was it the only time he'd been punished for a crime he didn't commit. The second instance, she knew all too well because she was the one who'd done the accusing when all Tobin had done was the right thing.

She kicked a rock, sending it into the shadows. Tobin was Tobin. He hadn't changed. The scary thing was how much she had — and how she'd never noticed until now. She'd gotten colder. Harder. Judgmental, like everybody else.

The kids who'd tagged along chattered away at Tobin, and he chattered right back in nonsensical syllables that made them giggle and tease.

She wanted to stop him there and then, scream and shout. At him, at herself.

Tobin! Why did you let me go? Why didn't you come back to me?

That one, she knew the answer to. She'd told him she never wanted to see him again, that's why. Yelled it at the top of her lungs.

She was the one who'd ruined everything, not him. He was the one who ought to be asking her, *Cara, why didn't you come back to me?*

It had all seemed so black and white, until everything faded to a thousand shades of gray.

"Listen, Tobin," she started, trying to get the words organized in her mind. *About us. About six years ago when—*

He held up a hand and gently shushed her. "Listen."

The sound of the waterfall broke through the trees, and a patch of sunlight pierced the foliage ahead. "We're nearly there."

Her mouth closed. Opened. Closed again, and stayed that way.

A minute later, they really were there, and even the straight-faced bushmen accompanying them stood in a reverent kind of daze.

The waterfall fell from sixty feet above, scraping a half bowl out of a yellow-brown cliff. Somewhere above it were the upper two stages of the falls. Unobstructed sunlight filled the clearing with golden light, and rainbows played in the mist. Cara couldn't resist turning her face up to the sky, soaking the sun in after nearly a week spent in shadows.

"You don't realize how much you miss something until it's gone, do you?" Tobin asked in a hushed voice.

She glanced over and found him looking at her, not the sun. His lips quivered, and part of her wanted nothing more than to lean toward him and find out what those unspoken words might be.

Then he flipped a switch and went back to fun-loving Tobin. "Coming in?"

He strode toward the edge of the pool, shedding layers as he went. He dropped the shoulder bag on a stone, spread his shirt across a bush. He'd changed into a pair of surf shorts back in the village — unlike her, the man had the foresight to bring a backpack of things. He stood before her, tan, tough, and bare-chested, and held out a hand. "Come on!"

She folded her arms. "I don't have anything to wear."

His eyes sparkled. "So don't wear anything."

Click, zing. Caption: *The zest of life.* The man was one of a kind.

"What about them?" She jabbed a thumb over her shoulder at their escort.

"Who?"

She spun around and found nothing. Their escort had disappeared into the foliage.

"I think they're off hunting. Just you, me, and the kids now."

She looked over to find the two little boys already making for the shallows.

She blinked. If the guards were gone, maybe she and Tobin could make a run for it.

"I doubt they're far," Tobin said, reading her mind. "Now's not our chance to escape. Not yet. But it is our chance for a nice, refreshing dip. Come in, already."

God, the water was tempting.

"It's probably full of leeches," she protested, wondering why she was trying so hard to say no.

"It's clean. Fresh. You know how good this feels after months of salt water?"

No, she didn't, but she hadn't washed properly in days, and everything itched.

"Come on, Cara!"

Tobin didn't wait. He just turned and made for the pool. He'd pulled the same trick the first day they met, leaving her at the lip of a slope and skiing away. And silly girl, she'd followed right him down that mountain. Then another and another, and eventually, she'd followed him right into bed.

And damn it, the same magic was working on her now, because she already had the buttons worked halfway down her shirt. Most of the women in the village went topless, so surely, she could strip down to panties and a bra. And no one was looking, right?

Except Tobin. He'd already plunged in, surfaced, and turned, watching her pull off her shirt, then peel down her lightweight khaki pants. Watching her the way he watched waves breaking off a beach, waiting for his chance.

She sucked in a deep breath, studying the water. It looked deep. Dark. What exactly was she getting herself into here?

Cara. Come in. He didn't say it, but she could feel him pushing the thought her way.

Temptation pulled at her. Tobin. Cool, beckoning water. Tobin, again.

She closed her eyes and jumped in.

Chapter Thirteen

Except for treading water, Tobin stayed very still, afraid to spook her into shying away. His mind was a little stuck, too, at the sight of Cara considering that jump. Her nipples strained against the cups of her bra, her hair bounced as she bobbed her head in indecision.

He ought to feel guilty, but it wasn't like he'd *planned* to lure her into a perfect freshwater pool at the base of a gorgeous waterfall in this overgrown Garden of Eden. He couldn't help the thought that fluttered through his mind as she jumped.

Adam, meet your Eve.

And that's what she was — the only woman in the world. It had been that way since the day they met, when he'd done everything he could to resist getting sucked in by that girlish innocence — and failed just as miserably as he was failing right now. He was supposed to be figuring out an escape plan, not getting off on the sight of her body. A good thing the water was cold, or he'd be trying to tread water with a foot of wood between his legs.

So when she surfaced next to him, water streaming in tiny rivers along her ebony hair, he did the only logical thing: stroked away from her, because otherwise he'd be stroking some part of her body, and that just wouldn't do.

That crazy magnetic pull that always drew the two of them together hadn't let up one bit, and that just made her harder to resist. Cara felt it, too. He knew from the way she'd touched his cheek back in the village, seen it in the looks she averted a second too late during the long walk. Heard the waver in her voice the few times she'd spoken to him in between. Yeah, Cara was about as over him as he was over her.

Which was good, right?

His heart was doing backflips, going *Yip yip yip* like an overexcited puppy, but his mind knew better.

Watch it. Danger. Heartache ahead.

If he got his hopes up, they'd only be dashed, and the only thing worse than having Cara walk away from him once would be Cara walking away from him a second time.

He swam a little farther, not looking back, trying to force his mind back to his plan. So what if they were half naked in a waterfall? So what if she looked like a goddamn portrait of Venus, streaming water as she emerged from a shell?

He gulped a huge breath of air and dove. Deep, and forward, to where he could feel the waterfall pounding away. Forcing his eyes open, reaching around with his arms. Trying to judge how much depth they had and how much they needed for his crazy idea to work. Came up for air, calculating exactly where he was in the basin.

He'd been careful to keep his bearings as they hiked in. The roaring river wasn't far downhill, and the bridge was somewhere to the left. That meant the place where he'd stashed his bike was somewhere downslope from this spot at the foot of the waterfall.

All within reach, if he calculated it right. Somehow, he and Cara would have to make it back here without the escort. But he had a plan for that, too. A crazy one.

He looked up at the waterfall. Crazy worked surprisingly well half the time. The other half... Well, it was one thing to risk his own neck. Another thing to risk Cara's.

He dove again, keeping his eyes open. He couldn't see far, but at least it didn't sting like salt water did, back when he'd had to dive to clean *Serendipity's* hull. Five powerful strokes and he still hadn't hit bottom. Six. Was it deep enough?

He darted back to the surface and popped out right next to Cara. So close, that he practically came up between her arms.

So close, that for a minute, everything fled his mind. The escape plan, the calculations, the estimations of speed and time. It was just him and her and the panting breaths he was still heaving after staying under that long.

Back to the plan, idiot. Back to the plan.

Tobin. Her lips moved, though no sound came out.

Before he did something dumb, like kiss her, he backed away. A couple of strong strokes got him around the outside edge of the pulsing stream. Two more and he snuck behind the curtain of the cascade. The roar of falling water grew muffled and the temperature immediately dropped ten degrees. Keeping the solid rock of the cliff to his back, he watched the silvery screen of water flow, nearly solid but for flickering glimpses of green foliage or blue sky. A cool, quiet little den to hide away in and get himself together. To remind himself that this was about her, not him. Not *them.*

But there was a dream-like quality to that little scoop of air behind the waterfall. Enough that when the water before him darkened, then split as Cara entered his secret realm, he was slow to react. When he did, it was too late, because she swam right into his arms.

Their limbs acted on instinct and intertwined before his mind had any say in the matter. Because, yeah, he could live to a hundred and two and never forget how to hold Cara. Didn't seem that she'd forgotten either, because she went straight into a hug and a straddle that begged him to pull her closer still. Each of them leaned forward for a kiss that was just like the waterfall: all power, all nature, all gravity. They met exactly in the middle, so it wasn't him doing it and it wasn't her. It was them, like *them* was its own living force with a mind of its own.

The kiss was sad and bright and hopeful, all at the same time, and it sucked him in.

Part of his mind tried to protest. *This is about her. Not her and me.*

But his body screamed, *Us, us, us!* and he couldn't let go.

Coming up for air was an afterthought, and they both gasped and blinked.

"What was that for?" he managed. Sneaking up with kisses was supposed to be his job.

She bent her forehead to his and stayed there a good long time.

"For old time's sake," she whispered, barely audible above the roar of the waterfall.

Old times. His heart ached just thinking about it.

"Tobin," she whispered. "I wish..."

He let the sentence drift away, unfinished. Yeah, he knew all about wishes and regrets and how much they hurt, even when left unsaid.

Then Cara tilted her chin up, shook her head, and dove in to another kiss.

Her lips were soft, her breath sharp, her hips tight against his waist. The roar in his ears got louder, as if someone had just turned up the volume on the waterfall. She tasted every bit as good as she had six years ago. Or even better, because he was hungrier now. Sadder. Smarter. Or dumber, because Christ, what was he doing?

He squeezed as tightly as he dared, pressing her breasts flat against him so their hearts had a chance to do their own little cha-cha like their lips were doing one story up. If his eyes were open, nothing was registering there, because it was all the taste, the feel, the heat building a fire between them that the water of a thousand gushing rivers couldn't put out.

The water was pure. Soft. Cleansing. Maybe if they stayed there long enough, it would wash the past away.

"Tobin," she mumbled, her lips tickling his. "We really need to talk."

"You talk, I'll kiss," he murmured into her ear.

"Tobin, all of this..."

She trailed off when he started nibbling his way down her neck. He couldn't help it. Sure as a siren, she was drawing him in. The curve of her body, the soft skin... He'd almost started believing that reality couldn't be as good as the memories, but it was every bit as good. Better, even.

His heart soared when Cara let out a little moan. Her lips moved again, her voice a whisper above the roar of the falls. "Tobin, you and me..."

"You and me," he agreed, running his hands down her sides. Scooping her closer into his lap. God, why hadn't he gone after her in all those wasted years?

Because she'd been pretty clear in expelling him from her life, that's why. But up here in the jungle, far from her office and job, she was opening up again. Letting herself live and love for a change.

He let his hands explore her back, then trace her sides to the curve of her breasts. She arched into him and dragged her lips from his mouth to his ear, making hungry sounds. His cock was rock hard and jutting into her, and if he just tilted a tiny bit forward—

"Hola!" came a squeaky voice in the foreground of the waterfall's din.

His eyes popped open, and Cara's, too, and both of them turned to the little boy wearing a wide grin.

"Amigos!" the boy said, oblivious to what he'd just interrupted.

"Hola," Tobin groaned. A ripple of protest went through every muscle, every joint.

Cara buried her face in his shoulder, and though it wasn't exactly what his body ached for, it was still a minor thrill. She hadn't splashed and rocketed off his lap when she realized just how close they'd gotten, right?

He crossed his arms over her back and held her close, making a silent promise to himself. *Will never let go. Will not fuck up. Not this time.*

Chapter Fourteen

One more kiss, and then he slipped away.

Cara watched Tobin vanish into the real world on the other side of the waterfall. Her whole body screamed for him to come back, but Tobin was gone.

The feeling wasn't, though. The feeling that part of her could only breathe when Tobin was close. That an extra chamber of her heart had gotten into gear along with a whole new set of nerve endings that sparked and cried and came to life.

Holy Mary and Joseph, the man could kiss.

Tobin kissed the way he lived: all out, all heart, everything on the line. And the shine in his eye afterward swore that he only did that for her. No lies, no stories, no intrigue.

He was so easy to trust. But the minute her mind got back in gear, it felt awfully complicated to let herself love the world's least complicated man. Especially with a dozen doubtful voices echoing in her mind.

He's no good for you.

Why can't you find someone more like his brother?

A man like that is bound to cheat on you sooner or later.

Her stomach had fluttered with butterflies a minute ago; now it sank like a stone. Maybe she'd heard those lines so often, she'd started to internalize them. The same way Tobin did with all the deprecating comments he turned into jokes.

She cupped a handful of water and let it drain slowly over her face. They were words, only words. Words had a way of tangling a person up until she was trapped in a net of her own making.

"Señora! Señora!" The little boy waved eagerly for her to follow and dove out of that hollow behind the falls.

With a deep breath, she followed. But she must have shot off at the wrong angle because this time, the waterfall pounded on her back and drove her under.

She kicked and stroked, but the crushing force was too strong. The light dimmed as she was driven into darker, colder water. She kicked harder, trying to escape the pounding at the center of the falls, but got nowhere.

Down? Up? She squinted, trying to orient herself. The water foamed and bubbled all around. Her kicks grew more frantic, less coordinated with her flailing arms.

Tobin! She wanted to scream.

She was just starting to panic that maybe she couldn't do it when the pull released her — reluctantly. Two hard kicks — the kicks of her life — and she popped up to the surface, gasping for air.

She spent a long time blinking the water out of her eyes. The little boy was over on the edge of the pool, smiling and splashing without a care in the world. So he was all right. But what about Tobin?

She scanned the pool. Oh God, where did Tobin go?

Then he popped up — way up and out of the water, shooting up like he'd descended to lung-crushing depths — and heaved a couple of huge breaths. His eyes weren't wild or worried, but calculating. Then he gulped some more air and dove out of sight again.

She let out a long, wavering breath.

It figured Tobin had it all under control. Just the way he mastered the steepest ski slopes, the biggest, craziest waves.

He dove over and over, until he finally took a break and went to floating on his back, eyeing the waterfall. Not appreciating it or catching it for a mental album — caption: *Beautiful waterfall where Cara jumped my bones* — or marveling, but calculating. What he was thinking, she couldn't tell. Only that he was a man possessed with a mission of some kind.

Typical Tobin. Her dad called him lazy, but that wasn't it. He was choosy, very choosy about what he put his passion behind. And right now, his passion seemed firmly fixed on exploring the depths of the pool beneath the waterfall, not on demanding that she explain whatever impulse it was that had her doing a lap dance on him behind the waterfall. As if she could explain, even to herself.

She swam back to the edge of the pool, clambered out, and sat on a rock in the sun next to his backpack. Chilly from the water, she rummaged in the bag for the little hand towel she'd seen him pack. She pulled it out and blotted at the water on her face.

Her foot knocked the backpack over, and her eyes caught on a book.

Last she remembered, Tobin had been into submarine adventure novels. Had his tastes changed over the years?

She pulled out the book and decided, nope. Not much. It was a worn paperback that looked like it'd been through a thousand hands. There was a square-rigged ship on the cover and a lot of exclamation points in the description. Judging by the glint of hero's sword and the size of the heroine's boobs, there was plenty of action between the covers *and* between the sheets.

She couldn't hold back a smile. Maybe Tobin would let her read it when he was through.

Which, judging by the placement of his bookmark, wasn't far off. She cracked the book open there, trying to guess what she'd find.

Something like *"Arrr," cried Captain Jack as he swung from the mizzen to the deck.* Or maybe, *Claudette brandished the cutlass and screamed as she leaped to his defense.* Or maybe—

She stopped short. Not at the chapter opening, but on the bookmark — a photograph. A familiar one.

She gulped and looked up, afraid Tobin might catch her snooping, but he was still swimming, diving, engineering something in his mind. Clueless that she'd just found the picture he still carried after all these years.

The picture of the two of them on top of a white mountain in winter. Their cheeks were rosy, their grins a mile wide. They looked a little younger. A lot happier. And absolutely, unmistakably in love.

She turned it over, already knowing what the message on the back said, because she'd read what he'd penned there that Valentine's day long ago, and dozens of times after.

A year ago we met on this very mountain and you changed my life. I'll love you forever, Cara. Will you be mine?

When he said *mine*, he meant it, because he'd gotten down on the snow on one knee and asked if she would marry him.

She brought the hand towel back to her face to catch the extra moisture dripping down her cheeks.

Yes, Tobin, yes. I'll be yours forever.

She'd added that part underneath later in the day, when they made it back to the bottom for the candlelight dinner he'd arranged.

On that February day, everything had been so perfect. And when she thought it over, everything about the six months that followed was pretty perfect, too. Right up to the awful day she'd screamed and cried and thrown that picture back in his face.

Go, Tobin. Leave. I never want to see you again.

She'd shrieked that part, and he stood there looking like a lost puppy who had no clue about his crime. He might have stood there a whole lot longer if her dad hadn't barged in and thrown not just a fit, but a couple of chairs, too. All aimed at a man who'd cheated on his bride two days before his own wedding.

Except Tobin hadn't cheated. He hadn't lied.

She swallowed hard, and it echoed in her ears. She was slumped over her knees by then, rocking herself and wishing none of it were true. The pain she'd felt when she thought he cheated was nothing like the hurt he must have felt at being accused. By her.

"Heya, Cara," he shouted from the water.

She snapped her chin up and flipped the book shut. "Yeah?" It came out weak and warbly.

"You okay?"

He was treading water, looking at her from thirty yards away. Checking if she was okay. He'd stopped everything he was doing and come halfway across the country to check if she was okay.

Tobin had never, ever let her down. And he never, ever would.

Was she okay?

Kinda. Sorta.

If she was okay, it was only because he was here, promising her everything, asking for nothing.

She sniffed and looked at him and managed a weak smile. Then she pointed the camera of her mind's eye at the waterfall and captured the scene. *Click!* Caption: *The man that I loved.*

The minute the thought slipped out, she wanted to correct it. *The man I still love.*

Chapter Fifteen

Where the rest of the day went, Tobin wasn't sure, but it passed in a blur. A wordless picnic lunch at the base of the falls, an hour of wondering why Cara was so quiet. Then the guides-slash-guards had reappeared and led the way back along the rough jungle trail.

An hour of walking stretched into two, and his mind kept skipping between what he'd already started to think of as The Waterfall Kiss and The Great Escape. One second, he'd be calculating angles and heights and likeliness of instant death, and the next, he'd go hot all over and relive the moment when Cara slid into his lap and wrapped her legs around him. He ached to have her that close again. For her to put her lips on his and mumble, *Yes, yes, yes.*

Slowly, gradually, another image edged in. A long-forgotten one that tickled the back of his mind, drifting in and out of focus as he ducked under low-hanging leaves and vines. The more he concentrated on it, the more the jungle faded away. And there it was: his Grand Plan.

It was going to be a wedding surprise for Cara: him buying into a local ski hill and settling down. The plan had pretty much self-imploded six years ago, as he had. And yet there it was again, dancing in the shadows of the rain forest. His business plan.

Yeah — him, Tobin Cooper, with a business plan.

He'd had it all figured out. The place he'd learned to ski as a kid had been abandoned for years. It wasn't much — just a single bunny hill with a rusty T-bar. But it didn't have to be much. The place was close enough to the outer Boston suburbs to guarantee business, even in tough economic times.

A lift pass at a place like that cost about as much as a Happy Meal, so it would be cheap, close, and convenient. Customers guaranteed, and a lot of joy for a lot of people. Just the kind of business venture Cara had always encouraged him to explore.

He'd planned it, A to Z. Even got a bank to okay a loan. On the way from the wedding to the honeymoon, they would stop by Beech Tree Hill so he could show Cara the place, reveal his plan, and watch her swell with pride. They'd look out over the hill and laugh and hug and picture their own kids learning to ski there someday.

His thoughts skidded to a halt there. So, okay, that would never happen. But the rest... It would be a good business. Small enough for him to keep a handle on, big enough to make a living off. The clients would be happy. And him, he'd be happy enough.

Squeaks and squawks came from the jungle canopy, reminding him where he was. Why.

Cara. Everything he'd ever wanted, and still did.

Her hand was there, just asking to be held, so he did. Held it the rest of the way back into the village, in fact, and reveled in every second that ticked by with her fingers laced through his. His mind jumped time and place, hopping between a wintery New England and this Central America jungle, and he wondered. Wondered a bit too much for his own good.

Then a mosquito buzzed in his ear and he mug-slapped himself back to figuring how far they might run and how fast. Because tomorrow was the day. Friday.

Tomorrow he had to get her out of here. All they needed was an early start and a little luck.

Until then, they had what was left of the afternoon and a very long night. How the hell was he going to be able to crawl into bed next to Cara and not do all the things his body craved? Like kissing her senseless, then making his way down her perfect body and kissing some more. Relearning every inch of Cara until she was moaning, begging for him to let her come. Then he'd slide inside and the two of them would soar like a couple of birds—

"Butterflies, *señor?*"

He blinked. They were nearly back at the village. Rodrigo stood before him, asking about...what?

"Did you see any butterflies?" Rodrigo asked, scrutinizing him for any hint of a lie. Yeah, he knew Tobin was up to more than just vacationing with his almost-wife.

So he told the truth. Or a half-truth, anyway. "Honestly, I kind of lost track. Spent more time watching my beautiful wife."

My wife. It had a ring of rightness to it.

Forget the bugs, the humidity, the rain shower just starting to trickle through the thick canopy above. He had his woman. His wife.

Okay, his almost-wife.

Their walk became a run as little sprinkles of rain turned into heavy drops and then solid sheets, putting the rain back in the rain forest and urgency back into their step. They sprinted into the village and ducked under the open-sided building that served as communal space. He skidded to a halt, laughing, and caught Cara in a hug. Let the water drops slide between their bodies. Let the rain pound down. He had her and—

Cara pulled back with a sharp breath.

"Ca—" he started to protest. Why did she have to fight something that felt so right?

But her eyes weren't on him. They were wide and frightened, focused on a distant corner of the open space.

The hair on the back of Tobin's neck stood up and he whirled, instinctively stepping in front of Cara.

"*Buenos días,*" said a gritty, greedy voice.

Nobody answered. Not any of the village elders, huddled pensively to one side. Not the hunters, who eyed the newcomer like a venomous snake. Not even Rodrigo, who'd stepped into the shelter behind them and came to a sudden halt.

Except for the rain, there was no noise at all. Not the friendly chatter of women at work, nor the lilting voices of children at play. Not even curious faces peeking out of doorways. The entire village was hushed.

"*Buenos días,*" the newcomer repeated. Not a greeting. A command.

"Buenos días," a few voices murmured on cue.

Tobin glared. Who was this jerk?

Che Guevara on a very bad day didn't begin to describe the man. Scrappy beard, unruly locks of hair. Dark, darting eyes. His jungle camos weren't just soaked; they were filthy. A cigarette drooped from his lips, the rancid odor so out of place in this lush, green space. He sat on a log in the shelter, a rifle slung at his side. He shifted a leg and the barrel swung right at the elders. A carefully calculated move, or sheer carelessness?

"Alfonso," Rodrigo muttered between clenched teeth.

Tobin curled an arm backward, keeping Cara behind him. Wrong move, because the movement caught that man's gaze and focused it right on Cara.

"Buenos dias." The man's voice rose, buttery and soft. His eyes, though, were that of a cobra, studying its prey.

Cara stiffened behind Tobin's back, and her fingers clenched his so tight, it hurt. Not that he was planning on letting go anytime soon. Not with that asshole hanging around.

Tobin narrowed his eyes and channeled *jungle warrior* at the intruder. It was obvious the intruder wasn't welcome in the village. The men all stood stiff; the women chewed their lips and shot uneasy looks at one another.

A drug runner? What else could this grub of a man be? He wasn't one of the bridge guards, that was for sure. Latino, not *indigeno*, like the villagers were. An outsider.

A dangerous one.

"Alfonso!" All heads snapped right, to where Lefebvre wandered in and gave the intruder an encouraging slap on the back. His eyes were glassy, his gait not quite right.

Tobin looked from one to the other. The anthropologist was buddies with a drug runner?

Alfonso, the newcomer, handed Lefebvre a tightly wrapped bundle. Pot? Cocaine? Whichever it was, it explained their unlikely friendship. A dangerous friendship, Tobin decided. Even the poker-faced villagers scowled, observing the two.

An older women shuffled forward with a liquid-filled gourd, but Alfonso pushed it away, snarling. *"Chicha! Chicha fuerte!"*

The old woman kept her eyes down and beat a hasty retreat as a spirited protest ensued. Rodrigo, the elders, and the trio of village huntsmen all started talking at once. Tobin didn't have to speak their language to get the message. No chicha. No way.

He'd tried a swig of the stuff once, back in Catalina, and he could still taste the burn in his throat. The last thing this unwanted visitor needed was a shot of alcohol in his system. Tobin could smell the dope on him, see it in his bloodshot eyes.

The eyes that had stopped roving and settled squarely on Cara. Appraising. Hungry. Crude.

Tobin shifted right and socked the man with the evil eye. *Just mess with me, asshole. Just try.*

The man stared right back and slid a hand to his gun.

Chapter Sixteen

Alarms sounded throughout Cara's body, ringing, blinking, and whooping. It seemed as if every man in the village glared at Alfonso from the shadows. The women were on guard, and every young girl was conspicuously hidden away. Even if this stranger hadn't been in her field of vision — or had been, until Tobin moved to block him out — she would have felt him there. The way you felt a stranger walk behind you on a dimly lit street, or a mean mutt eye your ankles, calculating how far his chain might let him reach. That's what the man was doing now. Calculating.

One gun against a dozen visitors — plus Tobin, who stood before her like a brick wall. He seemed to have doubled in size, a silverback gorilla ready to defend his turf.

The terrifying thing? *She* was the turf, and a fight could mean death.

Part of her wanted to huff, flip the intruder off, and put these posturing men back in their places. Who did this Alfonso guy think he was, looking at her like that? And who did Tobin think he was, playing knight?

Another part of her, though, shrank away. The scene playing out in front of her wasn't just posturing; it was the prelude to a fight.

Something tugged at her hand. The old woman, motioning her away. Urgently. Insistently.

Come with me. Now. Get out of this bad man's sight.

Nothing she'd like better, but she wasn't going anywhere without Tobin. She pulled his hand, and he turned.

Her breath stuck in her throat, because it was a Tobin she'd never, ever seen before. Gone was the generous charm, replaced by a fierce, intent warrior, ready to lay it all on the line. For her. Nostrils flaring like an angry bull.

She tightened her grip. If fingers could talk, hers would be begging. *Tobin, come with me.*

His eyes flashed. *You go. I stay, as long as this shit stays.*

No way. *Not without you.* No way was she leaving him in a stare-off with an armed man.

His eyes flickered, softened, and then closed briefly. When they opened again, he brought her hand to his mouth and kissed her knuckles. The lapis blue eyes gazing into hers were full of promises and hopes, and something inside her melted as her heart begged for permission to love him again.

A second ticked by, and in it, an eternity. The intruder and the village and the rain forest all blurred out of focus until it was just the two of them.

Then something moved at the periphery of her vision, and she snapped back. Rodrigo and his uncle — bless them — had stepped in front of Alfonso, continuing their protests.

"No chicha! No!"

That gave her the break she needed. Cara pulled on Tobin's hand, and this time, he followed her back out into the rain.

It was a cleansing rain that scrubbed the doubt and desperation away until she'd never been as sure of anything in her life as she was sure of him. Of them. A rain that chased them right across the clearing, splattering mud as they ran for the bungalow that felt surprisingly like home. She ducked into the doorway. Tobin was right on her heels, so close that his chest covered her back like a sheet of armor.

He pushed the door closed and they stood looking at each other. Chests heaving, water dripping, with a thousand unspoken words hanging in the thick air.

Tobin dragged his eyes off hers and stooped to look out the tiny window cut into the woven-mat wall.

She gulped away what she was about to say and peered outside.

"What do you think?"

The sinews of Tobin's throat flexed and strained. "A drug runner, for sure." He turned back to her. "Jesus, Cara, what was your company thinking, sending you up here alone?"

When he put it that way, it did sound pretty careless. She bit her lip. "I had a guide. I was expecting it to be in and out. Just one afternoon."

Tobin shook his head and stared out the window. The rain hammered on the roof as she sorted through it all. How a single afternoon had somehow become a week. How a business trip into the jungle had somehow turned into a voyage through memories, emotions, and regrets. All the things she'd kept locked up, suddenly thrust into daylight, begging to be resolved. Here, of all places — this tangled, primal place.

Without thinking, she dropped her head to Tobin's shoulder and laid a hand flat on his chest, feeling the steady thump of his heart, and closed the world away. Listening.

Thump.

Thump.

Thump.

His breath was a whisper on her cheek, his body solid steel. She, meanwhile, was a melting, soggy mess.

His arm curled around her waist, warm and tight. Right. The pounding of rain eased to a slap, then splattering drops. Tobin's chest rose and fell with every breath.

"He's leaving." Tobin nodded, or maybe growled.

She cracked her eyes open and looked out. Back into the real world, where Alfonso sauntered off into the jungle as if there weren't a dozen angry tribesmen ready to aim their blowguns at his back. She could swear his look said, *I'll be back,* Terminator-style. His rifle bobbed with every step until the foliage swallowed him up.

"God, I wonder how often they have to deal with him."

Tobin shook his head sadly. "Too often, I'd say."

She shivered and he hugged her tighter. Like a cat who'd finally wandered home after being lost, she snuggled right into her old spot. Nose to his neck, ear to his cheek. Right there where problems fled and everything felt peaceful and safe. All the more when Tobin rested his head on top of hers and slowly let his stiff muscles loosen up.

"Mmm," he hummed.

"Hmm?"

"Nothing," he sighed. "Just mmm."

She looked up and found him smiling at her.

She flicked her fingers along his forearm. "You're wet."

"You're wetter."

She laughed. A good, resounding laugh that felt like a million bucks. "Am not."

"Are too," he scolded. "It's all this hair." He ran his fingers through her locks, sending warm tingles through her body. She closed her eyes and concentrated on the feel of him, that close. His fingers massaging her scalp, tucking her hair back into place.

"God, I'm a mess."

"I like you a little messy. It's cute."

Her heart skipped into a happy little dance. Maybe there didn't have to be anything complicated about loving him. About letting him love her all over again.

"Only you would find this cute," she murmured.

He looked at her, and his eyes danced. *Yes. Yes, I do.*

Chapter Seventeen

Tobin reached behind her. "Better dry you off."

He dabbed at her with the towel he'd found. Gently, carefully, he chased the rivulets of water that streamed over her face and down her neck. When he rubbed under her chin, she couldn't help but lean into him.

The rain tapped on the roof in urgent little bursts and splattered in the puddles building outside the thin walls. The whole rain forest hushed under the deluge.

She leaned closer and closer as he worked the towel over her shoulders and down her back. The sound building in her throat was part purr, part lusty growl, and the lean became more of a squeeze as she pressed her chest to his. Tobin's hands were magic, just like his voice. Just like his smile, his touch.

Then she wasn't just warm, but hot. Hungry. She smoothed her hands over his chest. Ran her fingers down until they found the hem of his shirt and worked it up. The wet cloth rolled reluctantly, and she could relate. If she were plastered that tight against his body, she wouldn't go without a fight, either.

"Let's get you out of these wet clothes," she whispered, peeling the shirt away. Underneath was a wall of taut, tanned skin, and part of her sighed, being this close to him again. This intimate. No banter, no jokes. Just a couple of lovers pushed by the same primal desire.

"Cara." His hands closed around hers, but she pulled free. Another inch of shirt gave way, revealing a flat, hard nipple backed by solid muscle. With it came the hot memory of the time they'd holed up in a Colorado ski hut and—

"Cara." His voice was low and a little rough.

I want this, Tobin. I need this. She almost said it, but caught herself just in time. Tipped her forehead to his shoulder and took a couple of deep breaths.

Me, me, me. God, when had she become so selfish?

His hands massaged her shoulders, telling her it was all right. That was the problem: Tobin made it easy to take, and take, and take. He gave everything, asked for nothing.

"I'm so sorry, Tobin." She shook her head against his shoulder — the next best thing to crawling into a hole and hiding in shame. Fighting back the tears welling up.

"Sorry for what?" he whispered. The man's warmth was a drug, but she knew she had to resist. Had to finally get this out and get it right.

"Sorry for everything," she mumbled. Truly everything. "Making you come out here to help me," she started.

He smiled, and her hair shifted under his cheeks. "You could be in Timbuktu and I'd come for you."

He meant it. God, he really meant it. She blinked, and the first tears made their escape.

"Not just that." She clutched his shirt tighter. "For everything. For not believing you. For yelling. For saying all those terrible things."

He went still, then rubbed his chin over her head. "I've heard worse." He tried a little smile, but it didn't fool her. What could be worse than what she'd said and done to him? All that, plus the things she hadn't said. Like *sorry* and *I love you* and *I never should have doubted you.*

"I'm sorry. So, so sorry." She was babbling a little now, caught in a mudslide of emotions that she'd locked away so long ago that she almost forgot they were there. Until Tobin brought them all back. The love, the laughter, the regrets. So many regrets.

God, if only she could go back and start all over again.

She looped her arms behind his neck and cried into his shoulder. Cried enough to put the rain cloud outside to shame, babbling the whole time. "I'm sorry, Tobin. So sorry."

"Shhh," he whispered, holding her close.

She shook her head. Six years, she'd denied him those words. It was time to make it up, or start making it up. Trying, at least. If only she could find something more powerful than words.

"It's okay," he whispered, running a hand over her back.

She shook her head. "It will never be okay."

"It will if you let it."

She looked up, jaw a little slack. There it was — one of those little tidbits of Tobin wisdom that popped out of nowhere and walloped her over the head.

He cupped her face with both hands and looked into her eyes. "It's okay, Cara. Let it be okay."

Was it really as simple as that?

Deep blue eyes promised her it was, even as her soul continued to wrestle with the idea.

He sighed a little, then brought the towel up to dab her cheek. "Now you're wet all over again."

She put her hands over his. "You are a prince. A true prince."

He threw his head back and laughed. Laughter like a ray of sunshine in a very dark place. "No prince."

"A prince. A gentleman," she insisted. Because there she was, clinging to him like a child to a teddy bear, while Tobin held back. She could feel the restraint, feel him quivering for more than just a comforting kind of hug. He'd been exactly the same, their very first night. One thin strand of valor tried desperately to put on the brakes while desire poured off him in waves.

His smile faded. "I've given up on gentleman. It just doesn't pay."

Her chest tightened, hearing the truth in his words. Doing the right thing had only gotten him stung, again and again. But even so, he didn't give up. That was the thing about Tobin: easygoing teddy bear on the outside, knight in shining armor within.

She nuzzled up, her cheek to his, and rubbed back and forth against the stubble.

"Mmmm." A happy humming sound came from his chest. "Nice."

Very nice, so she did it some more. Eased up on her death grip of his shirt and slid her hands across the intersecting layers of muscle on his back. The happy hum was coming from her now. She nosed his ear. He smelled so good. Felt so good to have him this close again.

"Beware, m'lady," he whispered. "There be dragons in there."

Her heart thumped harder. "You want me to stop?"

"Only if you want to stop."

Like that was going to happen.

He looked at her more intently than she ever remembered him doing before. A new and different Tobin. Wounded, even if he didn't admit it. Wary. She'd done all that to him.

But maybe, just maybe, she could undo parts of it again.

She rapped her knuckles gently against his brow. "Knock, knock. Let the other Tobin out."

His eyes were closed, his whole body still. Only his lips moved. "What other Tobin?"

The one who loves me, she almost said, but settled for something more neutral. "The one who knows just how to touch me."

The hand he'd left against her chest twitched, and a whole cheering section went off in her mind.

"The one who kisses me, over and over and over again," she whispered, running her lips along his jaw.

His cock jutted against her stomach. He nuzzled his chin along hers in a long, sensual scrape that left every nerve in her body humming. His defenses were crumbling — and hers, too. The regrets were still there, but the burning need for more contact was shouldering them aside.

She nibbled his ear just above the lobe. Was that still his favorite spot?

His head tilted to her lips; his mouth opened in a silent sigh of pleasure.

A trail of happy sparks went through her, kindling the desire for more. Much more. To make this man not just sigh for her, but sing and cry and dance. Like she used to do for him, and he for her.

"Touch you where?" he whispered.

She wiggled her butt against his hand. "Here," she whispered. "And there," she added, breathing deeply enough to make her chest rise into his hand.

He brushed the other hand down her ass, then back up, bringing her closer. Danced his fingers over her collarbone, then stroked her neck.

The rain was pelting down harder, but nothing could extinguish the fire inside her.

"Kiss me, Tobin." She was begging, but that was all right, because she'd long since swallowed her pride.

And about time, too, she decided. Pride only got in the way of passion. And life without passion was like life without Tobin: empty as a desert instead of being as full as a jungle that teemed with sight, sound, sensation. Like the sensation of his heart, beating so close to hers.

He tilted his face closer, and she begged again.

"Kiss me, Tobin."

The old Tobin would have chuckled and teased. This Tobin was serious. Aching. She could hear it in his whisper. "Where?"

"Everywhere."

Chapter Eighteen

Tobin forced his eyes open, just to know this was for real. Not a dream, not a fantasy, not a memory.

But it was real. So real, it hurt. Hurt in a way he wanted to go on forever. Cara, wanting him. Needing him.

Six pent-up years of needing him, judging by the way she rutted up against him, making everything in him yowl and roar. If she'd hooked up with other guys since then, they hadn't done much for her. Not the way he could. That's what her body was screaming: it was him, only him.

He knew because it was exactly the same for him. He hadn't been playing monk these last couple of years, but no one had ever managed to produce the high Cara did with just a kiss. A whisper. A fleeting touch.

"Cara," he said, begging right back. And then he got to work on *everywhere*, just like she wanted.

He slid his lips over hers and got lost there for a while, inhaling her swallowed moans, her sweet Cara scent. Trying hard not to grind his cock against her and let her do the grinding, which was more than enough. Or not quite enough, because he wanted to consume her, take her, have her, all in one bite.

Cara was way ahead of him on that count, though. Her fingers knotted in his hair as she kissed him so hard and deep, his lungs ached. He tried to pretend he had his shit together up until she ran her hands up his chest and went to work on his left nipple, sending fireworks up and down his spine. Cara Leoni, in his arms again. He threaded his fingers in her hair and tried not to squeeze her in too close, lest he break the magic spell.

Holding back, though, was a losing battle. More and more of his weight slid over until he had her up against the doorframe. His hips ground against hers, and Christ, he could picture it already. The door would give and they'd tumble out. *Splat* — right into a puddle of mud. The way things were going, though, they probably wouldn't even pause. They'd go right on kissing and touching and slopping around like a couple of randy pigs in the mud.

"What's so funny?" she murmured, catching his chuckle.

"I can just picture this door giving way behind you."

"Well, then," she said in a deliberately sultry tone, "time to trade places, hotshot." She spun a finger in the air.

Her body shifted, and his followed in a slow, sultry dance. When they'd turned far enough for him to have his back to the door, she squeezed him up against it and kissed him.

And kissed and kissed and holy crap, *kissed*. He clamped his hands over her delectable ass and hung on. Her hands were all over him, exploring. Remembering. Holding. She'd speed up, then slow down, and he lost track of all sense of time. All sense of everything, because there was only her, tickling his neck then half ripping off his shirt. Shoving his shorts down then slowly fisting his cock.

She drew back, and his lips worked in thin air for a moment, wanting her back.

"Cara," he started, then stopped. Her look was pure mischief. Pure desire.

She dropped to her knees in front of him, and his heart jumped half out of his chest.

"Jesus, Cara," he managed, and damned if his voice didn't squeak like he was still fifteen and using magazines to get this kind of high.

"You don't want this?" She looked up with those luminous eyes. Eyes with centuries of passion wrapped up inside, just waiting to be freed.

"I want, I want," he said, and that came out better. More like a growl.

"Good," she said, leaning closer. "Because I want, too."

The minute she said it, want slid over to need and his body screamed for more.

There was a puff of air, then the world's lightest kiss. Then a wider, wetter touch that could only be her tongue.

He dropped his head back against the door with a heavy thunk and slid his fingers into her silky hair.

"Cara—" he moaned, giving up any pretense of having his shit together. Not with Cara working him like this. Toying with the tip of his shaft, then taking him deep, deep — holy-shit-deep.

She could have said anything then. *Tobin, get on your knees and bark like a dog. Tobin, get over to the bed and let me tie you down.* He'd do it in a heartbeat. Anything for her. For this. This slice of heaven he thought he'd never, ever experience again.

She came up for a breath of air and murmured "Oh, yes," before closing over him once more.

Then it was him saying *Oh, yes* over and over as she worked him with those perfect lips, that clever tongue. What her mouth couldn't reach, her fingers made up for, circling, then squeezing, then letting up, the perfect interplay of a little too tight and more-please-more. He might even have said that, once or twice.

His eyes rolled back in his head, and the only thought that fit in his blissed-out mind was that the minute he did get his shit together, he'd make her soar as high as she was sending him now, and do it for hours. Make her climb until she was whimpering the names of all the saints her parents made her memorize in Sunday school — the ones she really, really shouldn't call to mind at a time like this. Then he'd plunge inside her, man inside his woman, and make her sing to heaven as he finished what she was starting. Then they'd lie there sweating and heaving and muttering *Hallelujah* and *Amen*.

Except right now it was him doing the muttering, the sweating, the heaving. He rocked on his heels, setting a rhythm she caught on to, and Christ, he'd never felt his balls go that tight, his cock that heavy or slick. She had both hands wrapped around his hips now, squeezing him closer, and though he'd been in the same position a couple of times, he hadn't felt anything this close to total meltdown ever in his life.

But he sure as hell wasn't going to come in the mouth of his Italian princess, so he hauled her up to her feet and crushed his lips over hers. A little harder than he intended, but that seemed to suit Cara just fine. She tasted like...like him, and that set off a raw, animal urge.

"Fuck, Cara."

"Oh, we'll get to that," she said, looking far too satisfied for a woman who hadn't yet gotten her share. "I promise you, we'll get to that. But right now, we finish this."

This was her pulling his hand down to his cock and finishing him off, both of them together. Her hand should have felt tiny under his, but she had all the power. She watched his face from an inch away as he thrust harder and harder into her hand.

Let her watch. Let her listen. If she caught even a tiny fraction of this high, he'd be okay.

He heard her giggle, then huff into his ear. "Gotcha, hot-shot."

"You had me from the very st—"

The very start, he'd meant to say, but it got cut off by the tsunami that swept him into coming, hot and hard and heavy, in her hand. She milked every last drop while he shuddered and groaned and finally went limp.

Cara whisked the towel over both of them then ran a hand up his chest and chuckled.

"Gotcha."

Chapter Nineteen

Cara tucked her nose into the hollow of Tobin's collarbone and breathed him in as he slowly came down from his high. That scent was pure Tobin — an ocean breeze mixed with a lush jungle flavor that he'd made into his signature blend.

Him. Tobin.

Hers.

She snuggled closer, not quite ready to meet his eyes. Where that blow job had come from, she had no idea. Maybe it was the jungle, calling out the primal need in her. Maybe it was the result of having felt so trapped and alone over the past days, or even the past couple of years.

Or maybe it was the power of two long-lost soul mates, united at last.

How she'd ever let him go or doubted him, she didn't know. Right now, all she felt was the driving need to hold on and never, ever let him go.

So she didn't, even when he bent, flexed, and cradled her against his chest. She didn't let go as he carried her to the bed, and she sure didn't let go when he leaned her back on the mattress. Wherever he went, she went, too.

Which led to a moment of wrestling with the mosquito net and the last of her clothes, plus a frantic dig in his bag for a condom. But even that they did together; she held the bag while he rooted around.

"I bet you Tarzan never had these moments," he frowned.

She snorted. "I doubt he did. That Jane was a prude."

"Gotta feel for the guy. It's not like he had a lot of options."

She glowed a little. God knew Tobin had all the choice in the world, but he wanted her. Her!

He crawled over her body and tucked the condom next to the pillow. "Me, Tobin. You, Cara."

"So show me your stuff, hotshot." She kept her voice playful, instead of blurting the uncensored version in her mind. *Yeah, show me. Show me hard, fast, and deep.*

Yep, her inner cavewoman had definitely taken over. And God, it felt good.

"Be careful what you wish for, princess of mine."

"What are you waiting for, my good knight?"

His lips quirked. "Just deciding where to start. Here?" His eyes stopped on her lips, and he rubbed a finger across the seam. "Or maybe here?" His hand ghosted over the left side of her torso, hovering a hair over her skin.

She cheated and sucked in a deep breath, thrusting a breast into his palm. Getting him off had her wound tighter than tight, and her body begged for release.

He chuckled, but skimmed on. "Or maybe here." His voice dropped an octave as his fingers tiptoed toward her mound.

"Everywhere," she whispered, arching into him.

He tilted an eyebrow at her, and it sent flames licking through her body. Little flames that shot off in all directions, then reunited in a single, raging fireball in her core. She was writhing under him now, spreading her legs, inviting him in.

"Tobin…"

"So impatient. Don't you know we have all night?"

Her inner beast nearly let out a yowl, but Tobin drowned it with a kiss. His lips made little rippling motions over hers, setting wild signals through her nerves. His hand toyed with her breast, scooping and shifting the soft flesh while his thumb brushed over the nipple, bringing it to a peak. She hadn't felt so high, so wild, so… electrified in years.

Something between a squeak and a moan escaped her lips. "Oh, that feels good."

His hand strayed lower and slid between her legs, parting her folds.

She murmured something that came out garbled and low.

"You like that." The corners of his mouth quirked up.

Yeah, she was unraveling at the seams, but at least she had the satisfaction of hearing his voice go raspy and deep.

"You like it, too," she managed. Right before he slid a finger inside and made everything in her sing.

"I do." He flashed a wicked smile and slid a second finger in. He moved them in wide, wet circles, around and around.

"Tobin," she groaned, not really sure what she wanted to say.

"Cara." His eyes went dark with unveiled desire.

His fingers slid deeper, faster, honing in on the spot that would shatter her while his thumb pressed harder on her clit. She closed her eyes, riding this roller coaster to the very top, ready for the thrilling drop on the other side.

"Tob—"

She got that much out before his teeth scraped over her nipple, and then she was flying on a wave that seemed to tumble all of her insides. Like falling off a surfboard and swirling around in the frothy aftermath. Only better. Way, way better. She shook with an orgasm that went on and on until the roaring in her ears dulled to the quiet whisper of waves rippling over a beach.

She swallowed a couple of times, because she hadn't come that hard or that long in...in...well, a very long time.

Tobin kept busy, fluttering little butterfly kisses all over her chest, and when she cracked an eye open, he flicked his eyebrows up and smiled.

"You like that." Just the sound of his voice lubricated her joints.

"I love it."

I love you, she almost said. Good thing she was still catching her breath.

The rain pattered on the roof as the shower eased away, and the bungalow was dim. Twilight had fallen in a rush. The jungle came alive with a thousand squeaks, squawks, and chirps. Another minute passed in blissful, boneless oblivion, and if his cock hadn't jutted into her hip, she may well have spent another hour lying there. But Tobin's touch was like an on switch, and just like that, she was ready for more.

She jackknifed up and searched between the pillows for the condom, then tore the package open with her teeth.

Tobin's eyes shone, and then he winked.

"Hungry, much?"

Cara shoved him back onto the mattress. She'd show him hungry.

"Starving." Not just for sex, she was starving for him. For them to be one.

His cock twitched when she touched it, then throbbed as she unrolled the condom slowly, enjoying every hard inch. It was strange, though, too, because when they got engaged, they'd switched from condoms to the pill, not wanting a single layer separating them.

Now, that layer was back. That separation. She blinked a couple of times to push the lump in her throat back down. She wasn't about to ruin this magic with regrets, so she ran her hand over his hard length, then swung into a straddle over him. Quickly, before she chickened out.

She leaned low and sucked his lower lip between hers, rubbing it back and forth. A trick she'd learned from him, because while he was distracted with that, she tugged his arms up high. Then she reared back to admire the view, keeping his arms pinned over his head.

Tobin Whitman Cooper, ski hunk, surf god, and part-time jungle explorer, stretched out under her like a prize. Grinning like a fool, as if he were poised at the top of a mountain of fresh powder, ready for the ride of his life.

He made a show of struggling free, but when she lowered herself onto him, inch by luscious inch, he gave up the charade and went perfectly still. Keeping piercing eye contact, even with his eyelids sliding to half-mast. His hands broke free and clamped over her hips, and she rode him like a pony, rocking and pushing and sighing with every desperate breath.

He bucked under her, and they moved in perfect time as she leaned back to take him deeper. Deeper. Putting her hands on his thighs as the ride grew frisky, making the angle better still. Then the pony became a bronc and she was hanging on for a wild ride, shaking and waiting and crying for release.

But release wouldn't come; she'd build higher and higher, then somehow lose her grip, and he backed off every time.

"Tobin," she pleaded.

"Just a second longer," Tobin breathed.

Endurance. Not a good thing.

"No, Tobin, now. Please."

A corner of his mouth twitched, and then he rolled in one swift, smooth move that reversed their positions. She was stretched under him, arms pinned over her her, and he was the one settling between her legs.

"Yes," she cried. "Yes."

They were close now, so close, and her body screamed for more.

But Tobin? Tobin drew it out. Teased his cock along her folds. Pushed in, only to pull back.

"God, Cara, you're so goddamn tight."

"Good tight? Bad?"

He groaned, closed his eyes, and rocked some more. "Good tight. Great. Perfect."

Which was pretty much what she felt. Perfect. Or close to perfect. If he'd just let go...

"Tobin, come—"

He slid right in, and a jolt of power shot through her body. His angle was perfect, the pressure on her G-spot just the right mixture of smooth and hard. A slow slide out, a deliciously hard push back in. When he started thrusting, she gave in to the rush of pleasure with a howling cry of need. Even Tobin seemed to lose it, because his rhythm skipped and jumped, like he couldn't decide if he wanted fast or slow.

"Fast," she hissed between her teeth and clamped down hard with her inner muscles.

"Cara!"

No man had ever cried her name like that. A plea, a promise. A command.

She did it again.

"Cara!" The sinew and muscle went tight along his shoulders as he came inside her with a series of hard jerks, rasping her name. She came a second later, shaking through a long, rattling high and a glorious series of aftershocks that went on and on. Right to the point where her eyes fluttered open and found the look on his face.

His eyes were closed, his mouth open. Chin up, head back, riding the last energy of that wave. Her head buzzed a little, because Tobin Cooper, smoothest operator in the Northeast, was coming undone. With her. Not just with anyone. Just her.

He swallowed hard and opened his eyes, pulling her into that promising blue horizon. Then he folded carefully over her and let his weight settle like the world's coziest blanket. The bed that had seemed impossibly small before was now just right. She lay perfectly still, perfectly happy.

"Jesus, Cara."

Yeah, that helped, too.

"You can say that again."

He smiled into her neck and mumbled it again. "Cara."

Not an inch separated them. Tobin was as close as she could have him. She sighed so deeply, her chest lifted his body up and down.

And like he said, they did have all night.

Chapter Twenty

"Cara." Tobin tapped her lips with his, but she didn't stir.

The roosters were crowing, a dog barking, some kids whispering outside. The village was waking up, though it wasn't quite dawn.

Dawn on Friday. He had to smile at that. The jungle had finally gotten the better of Cara and her New York sense of time. That, or their nighttime antics had finally worn her out.

The thought ought to have stretched his smile wider, but all he did was gulp. It was a lot like their very first morning together in that ski chalet. He'd been terrified that she'd wake up, realize what a crazy thing she had done, and beat a quick, red-faced retreat out his door. Because Cara wasn't the type to do quick and easy. That part was obvious from the second they'd met, when the sparks started to fly and she tried everything she could to resist. Him, too, because he'd promised himself he'd get everything right for this woman. Like taking it slow, really slow, making sure she knew she was more to him than another ski bunny on another slope.

But it had been impossible to resist, just like last night was impossible to resist.

It would be so easy to start all over again right now. Kiss her lips, run a hand along her ribs. Forget her presentation. Forget everything for the next couple of days. Just live. Love. Enjoy.

And he nearly did it, because staying in the rain forest until Sunday was a hell of a lot more appealing than rushing away on the wings of his cockamamie plan.

But he had a promise to keep. To her and to himself.

"Cara," he whispered, giving her shoulder a shake.

She mumbled and rolled into his chest. He froze in round two of a silent inner battle of cock-versus-mind.

"Cara, we have to get up." He pushed her gently away from his side. "Today's the day."

"What day?" she mumbled.

"Friday. And you have a presentation to make."

She blinked. *Presentation? What presentation?*

He smiled and dropped that into the memory bank for all the lonely years to come — the knowledge that he'd managed to capture Cara's body and mind for a whole entire night.

"Come on, sleeping beauty." He tried kick-starting his humor, even though it dug back on its heels. "Gotta go. Got an escape to pull off."

She sat up and looked at him like he was nuts. "You mean it."

He nodded. "Of course I mean it." It might kill him to let her go at the end of this day, but yes, he meant it. He'd do what he promised to do.

They dressed quickly, then walked out at an agonizingly slow pace. If the villagers caught on to them now, they'd be sunk.

So Tobin smiled and played with the kids and licked his lips over breakfast, pretending he didn't have a care in the world. Cara did, too, and she was a champ, playing it cool. When he packed his backpack, he left a couple of things behind to make it look like they'd be back soon. And then they set off, down the jungle trail.

"Wait!" Rodrigo's voice shot out like a rifle behind them. "Where are you going?"

"The upper side of the waterfall, just like you said. Looking for butterflies," he said. Birds, butterflies, elephants. Whatever.

"Wait, you need a guide!"

"I know the way," Cara called, and it came out just right. Not too urgent, not too caring, nice and relaxed.

But Rodrigo stood glowering in the way, and they had no choice but to wait.

A butterfly fluttered overhead and Tobin barely noticed, entirely focused on what would happen when they got to the waterfall. The slowest minute of his life, because he had a deadline to make.

Finally, their guides jogged over, ready for a day in the jungle with their usual kit: loincloth, blowgun, nothing else. Cara gave him an anxious look, but he just shook his head. He'd been planning on them. Had been over the exact sequence of events a hundred times. The guides wouldn't stick with them — not the route he planned on taking, anyway.

He was about to step onto the path and go — finally go — when the bushes on the far side of the village shook. So hard, so loud that maybe elephant wasn't such a crazy image after all.

Then the bushes parted, and six men came out.

"Buenos días," the first one said.

For a split second, the whole village hushed. Then everyone scattered — women grabbing their children, hauling them out of sight. Girls first. Boys second. Men jumped to their feet and stepped toward the newcomers, just like the snarling dogs, then stepped back. You'd have thought Jesse James had just ridden into town and hopped off his horse the way the whole village tensed.

"Alfonso," Cara whispered in a shaky voice.

"Alfonso," Rodrigo spit out, his bronze skin going red.

"Alfonso and company." Tobin nodded, his mind freewheeling, trying to find a gear.

Because there wasn't just one desperado drug runner standing at the entrance to the village, but six. Six dirty men with rusty rifles and tangled hair. Their leader, a bearded Latino, doffed his cap with a nasty grin.

*"Amigos!"*he announced to nobody in particular.

Every villager dropped their eyes and clenched their fists.

Chapter Twenty-One

The village was silent as death. Even the roosters were quiet. Something caught on Cara's shirt, and she turned around.

A little boy stood behind her, tugging the fabric and waving her toward the waterfall path. One of the little boys who'd hiked with them yesterday. His eyes were making urgent signals toward the trail.

Let's go. Hit it. Now.

Sounded like a plan.

She caught Tobin's hand and squeezed until he turned around.

His lips were sealed in a grim line, his brow furrowed. The blood drained from her face, because Tobin didn't do furrowed or grim. Tobin did easygoing and relaxed.

Tobin was trying not to show it, but he was scared stiff.

The drug runners swept into the village with cocky arrogance, led by a tall man who kicked at a dog, gestured for water, and flopped down on the stool designated for the chief. Cara's skin crawled. If it were just Tobin there, he'd find a way to play the danger off. Share soccer scores, crack a couple of jokes, and tactfully turn down their offers of a drag of weed. They'd come, they'd go, no problem.

A white man in a rain forest village could get away with buddying it up with a gang of drug runners. A white woman, on the other hand...

The leader's eyes swept over the village and landed right on her. Skidded to a stop, was more like it. His gaze swept down, then up, lingering on her breasts. A broad grin crept across his face.

Her blood went cold. The feeling a jungle animal must get staring down the barrel of a blowgun. Staring down an ugly fate.

Alfonso stepped to the leader's side and gestured toward Cara. All six men looked her way. Their rifles dipped, momentarily forgotten.

One of them murmured something to Lefebvre, and he answered with a disinterested wave that said, *Take her. I couldn't care less.* Or maybe, *Teach these gringos not to come wandering too far off the beaten track.*

Tobin stepped in front of her, blocking her out of sight. He started stepping backward, muttering out of the corner of his mouth.

"Let's get going."

She could have strummed his voice and produced a note, it was strung that tight.

She turned for the path and took a couple of slow steps. Tobin was behind her, feeling his way into each backward step, refusing to take his eyes off the intruders.

A commotion broke out — the chief cutting the men off, judging by the sound of the ancient, brittle voice — and Tobin pushed her shoulder.

"Go! Go!" he grunted.

She broke into a trot, then an all-out run. Around the bend and down the trail, with the little boy flying along at her side.

The guides stuck with them, too, jabbering with each other in an urgent exchange.

Cara flew down the path just short of full tilt, because one misstep and a tree root would send her sprawling or a vine would grab at her shirt.

Tobin, by the sound of his footsteps, slowed down to look back, then hurried to catch up.

"Are they following us?" she shot over her shoulder.

"Not yet."

Yet.

She plunged on, wondering what was going on in the village. The drug runners looked surprised to see her, as if they hadn't believed Alfonso. They'd probably come to the village to squeeze a couple of free meals out of people who couldn't afford to say no to the hot end of a gun. Maybe they'd come looking for trouble, or what they might call fun.

Fun. She shuddered to think what their version of it might be. How they might want to include her in on it.

Tobin would try to stop them, but what could he do against six men with guns? Get himself killed, that's what he'd do. They'd shoot a dozen extra bullets into his body and then turn those hungry eyes on her...

"Faster!"

She forced her legs into a higher gear and sprinted down the narrow trail, hitting brush and oversized leaves as she fled. No time for a machete now; it was all about leaping, ducking, running full tilt.

Her breath came in heavy puffs, but she slogged on, wishing she'd thrown some sprints into her morning jogs back in Panama City.

She ran on and on. The rain forest was a blur of green, brown, and earthy black, the sounds of its inhabitants more urgent than ever. Gradually, the mumble of the distant river grew to a roar.

A roar punctured by a shout from one of the two guides as she flew around a bend and skidded to a stop on the edge of a cliff. A cliff opening on to the side of a waterfall. She held her breath and flapped her hands, tipping over the edge.

Tipping, tipping...

Her mind processed it all in slow motion. The tangle of blue-green jungle extending all around. The slopes of the river valley below. The cool rush of a river on her right, where it gushed over the lip of rock and plunged into nothingness. The space under her toes terrifyingly empty of anything but thin air.

She had just enough time to snap a mental picture and scribble a caption on it. *The End.*

Then something jerked her backward, and a strong arm wrapped around her waist.

"Holy shit..." Tobin murmured, dragging her back from the precipice, then mashing her against his heaving chest. His arms closed around her, and she hid in the den he created, trying to get her heart back in time with her lungs.

A deep breath, right against his shirt, and her trembling nerves filed slowly into place. She pulled back an inch and stared at the gap behind her, then at Tobin. They stood beside the first stage in the waterfall — a sheer cliff she'd nearly fallen off.

"Remind me to rescue you sometime, hotshot. I owe you." *Again.*

His eyes pooled a little before he crushed her in another hug. "You've got to stop getting ahead of my plan." Then he paused as if cuing a protest of some kind. Something like, *Plan? Tobin Cooper has a plan? Since when?*

She could practically hear the dismissive voices of his parents and hers. Them, and all the others who'd underestimated Tobin over the years.

She squeezed him even tighter and willed her thoughts into his mind. He was Tobin — her Tobin. Of course, he had a plan.

"Right," she said, letting him go. "Which way?"

He blinked and drew a long breath.

"That way," he whispered. Nothing moved but his lips, though.

A smile took shape on her lips, her cheeks, her whole soul. She whispered back. "I'm with you, *mi marido.* All the way."

His eyes glowed a little, but he didn't say a word. Just squeezed her hand tighter and gestured to the right. "This way."

They picked their way downhill, slipping and sliding down a muddy trail beside the waterfall. Then the slope bottomed out, and they emerged into a clearing. Tobin skirted a foaming pool of water and sloshed through ankle-deep water, right to the edge of another cliff.

The sun lit the way like a spotlight, and she joined Tobin on the top of the cliff. They were at the top of the third stage in the falls. Before her was a mighty view fit for a conquistador. She could picture the likes of Balboa standing there, sweating bullets and wondering if the jungle ever ended. The new bridge was a strip of gray to the left, the river a shining silver line edged with the browns of the ravine.

She looked up, back along the way they'd come. Two stages of the waterfall stretched above them. The third was in front of her where another cliff fell away, flooded by a gushing mass of water. At the bottom lay the pool she'd swum in the day before.

She peered down that final stage of the waterfall. At the very, very long drop.

"Um, Tobin? What exactly is the plan?"

Chapter Twenty-Two

Tobin edged forward and looked down.

Way down. Over a thundering waterfall that crash-landed into an emerald pool.

A hell of a long way down.

The drop looked even higher than it had the day before, when he'd been at the bottom. From down there, the pool looked bigger, the waterfall shorter. Now it was the other way around. The lake at the bottom looked like a kiddie pool, and the height had grown by a couple of stories overnight.

Cara squeezed his hand. "Um, Tobin?"

He couldn't bring himself to say it. He didn't need to, because half a second later, Cara caught a sharp breath and went tense all over. Yep, she had just figured out his plan.

"Um, Tobin, are you sure?"

He slid his jaw left, then right without answering. Yesterday, he'd been sure. This morning, he'd been sure. Now, he felt more like taking off in search of butterflies than following through with this crazy plan. He wouldn't even have to go far to find any, because he had a whole flock of them fluttering wildly in his gut.

He let out a slow breath and went over the plan in his mind. He'd checked the lower pool carefully. It was deep and free of jutting rocks. So, yeah, he was... kind of sure.

"We don't have to do this," Cara whispered, pulling him back. "It's not that important..."

The words set something off in him, because suddenly it seemed very important. Critical that he not back out now.

He tightened his fingers around hers and pulled her closer. "We can do this." It was a whisper, barely above the roar.

Her eyes were huge, her lip trembling.

"We can do this," he repeated, more to himself than to her.

One of the guides made a protesting sound behind him, and though Tobin didn't speak the language, he knew just what it meant. *Hey, mister, don't get so close to the edge.*

He looked down and gulped. *Maybe we don't have to do this,* his gut yelped.

A shout rang out and tore his attention away. A shout in Spanish, not the guttural local language, and he whirled.

He caught a glimpse of jungle camo, the gleam of a gun.

"Oh God," Cara murmured. "They're here."

His heart revved higher, right into the red zone, judging by the squeeze in his chest. The drug runners had caught up with them and were closing in.

"We have to do this," he said to Cara, turning back to the cliff.

He inched forward until his toes hung over the edge, even though his weight was well back. Cara stepped up beside him, curling and recurling her fingers around his.

"We just have to make sure we jump out far enough," he murmured.

The guide called again, more anxious now. *Hey, gringo! Watch that you and your woman don't go right over the edge!*

The drug runners yelled, too. *"Alla! Alla!"*

Over there! They're over there!

Tobin tightened the straps on his backpack and checked the quick release. If it started dragging him under, he could ditch it, but that was Plan B. Or C or D or whatever letter he was up to.

The commotion behind them grew louder. God, he really hated being rushed.

He leaned forward, keeping his weight right at the edge, and struck an even tone for Cara's sake. "Ready?"

Her answer nearly made him fall off the edge. "I love you, Tobin."

And somehow, he had an answer to that, even with the guides and drug runners screaming and splashing through the shallows toward them.

"I never stopped loving you, Cara." He took a deep breath and looked straight ahead. "Ready on three?"

He could hear her sharp inhale even over the rumble of the water. "Ready."

Just like going over the lip of a double diamond slope on an icy day, he lied to himself. He'd done it a thousand times.

"One."

An urgent string of syllables came from behind.

"Two."

Cara's hand clamped over his and he felt the men edge closer.

"Three!"

Chapter Twenty-Three

Cara had leaped off the high diving board at the YMCA. She'd even jumped off a rickety old pier on the New Hampshire shore when the tide was out, and that had seemed like a long, long way down. But that was nothing compared to the free fall she was in now.

The rush of falling water thundered in her ears. The spray was everywhere — under, over, around her. In her nose and mouth. She knew it wouldn't do any good, kicking wildly in the air like a cartoon character trying to get traction, but she did it anyway. But there was no traction, no way to get control. Only Tobin's hand to cling to and a wild prayer.

In the midst of all the overwhelming sensations threatening to short-circuit her brain, one thought struck her as particularly strange. How funny it was to be looking down on Tobin instead of up. He was ahead of her in the free fall, and a little farther to one side, and if she could have kicked her way over to cling to him, she would have.

The panicked intake of air she'd taken when she jumped didn't even last partway down, and she was forced to take a slurp of misty air in midjump. Even then she wasn't sure it would last the rest of the way.

"Shiiiiii—" he started to yell, but his voice cut off, and she made the mistake of taking another breath just as she hit the pool.

Impact was a whole-body punch that rattled every screaming joint in her body. The shock felt like a cold knife in her ribs, and she yelped, dragging in a lungful of water. She coughed and spluttered, trying to get her bearings. Which way was up? Everything was swirling and foaming around her.

She flailed in the dark water, fighting a sucking force that pushed her deeper, deeper. Too deep. Even worse, she'd lost hold of Tobin's hand. Where was he?

Pressure built behind her ears, along with the terrifying urge to inhale. God, she was drowning. It felt wrong, all wrong, to have survived the impact only to die that way.

She kicked, trying to claw her way up, but the force of the waterfall was keeping her down. Her mind flipped into panic mode. She'd never make it back up. She would drown. She'd—

A dark shape appeared ahead of her — Tobin! He'd help her and everything would be okay, right?

But something was wrong. Tobin wasn't moving, not fighting the pull. His arms were askew, his body limp.

Her heart wailed. They'd die here together, and for what?

She grabbed the back of his shirt, crying at the flood of pain in her lungs, ready to give up.

Give up?

A burst of heat went through her as she fisted his shirt and gave in to a screaming, stamping, full-out mental fit. No way was she going to give up! Not when everything depended on her. She owed it to Tobin to try.

No. More than try. She'd gotten him into this mess. She'd get him out.

Kicking upward was futile, so she tried kicking to the left. Kicking and scooping water with her free hand, keeping a death grip on him with the other. Tobin wasn't moving, either stunned by the impact or worse, knocked out. Her lungs wailed and her right arm twisted with Tobin's weight, but there was no way she would let go. Not now. Not ever.

She made a tiny bit of headway, but it was too slow. Her vision dimmed and went blurry around the edges.

Survival instinct screamed at her. *Let go of him! He's dragging you down!*

Her heart screamed right back. *Never letting go!* She screamed at her legs, too. *Try harder, damn it! Harder!*

She pulled and kicked until she thought she couldn't kick any more. Couldn't see, either.

One more kick! Just one more!

And just like that, she popped out on the surface, gasping and coughing and clutching at him.

"Tobin!" She meant to yell, but it came out in a choked whisper. "Tobin!"

She kicked toward the shore, dragging him along. On one stroke, her elbow struck his ribs, and Tobin started hacking and spitting and spluttering, too.

If she had an ounce of energy left, she'd have whooped. "Tobin!"

He blinked and coughed, red in the face but alive. Alive!

His eyes rolled upward, climbing the fall they'd just jumped. "Wow," he mumbled.

Cara glanced up to find the guides making panicked gestures before disappearing back into the forest. The drug runners were up there, too, pointing. Shouting.

Unslinging their rifles and taking aim.

"Go!" she yelped and dragged him right.

The water splurted in a tiny upward splash two yards away. She swam with all her might.

Another splash, another bullet. Closer this time.

She kicked behind the shelter of a boulder at the edge of the pool and yanked Tobin in.

Pling! A bullet bounced off the rock, and they both ducked.

"And I thought the fall was the dangerous part," Tobin muttered.

She balanced on a slippery underwater ledge and squeezed herself against the boulder. Kept her head barely above water level, as low as she could. She threw an arm over Tobin's shoulders and squeezed him in, too, as bullets zipped overhead.

Ping! Ping! Ping! Gunshots chipped off little shards of rock.

Ping! The water a few inches to her right jumped up.

She closed her eyes until the shots stopped, and even then kept them closed. Just in case.

When she worked up the nerve to open them again, Tobin was waving a tentative hand in the open, then peering around the boulder.

"They're gone."

She peeked, too. Nobody at the top of the cliff but one grinning little boy. Waving, like he'd just witnessed a really cool stunt and not two people fleeing for their lives.

Tobin waved back and started paddling to the very spot they'd climbed out of the pool yesterday.

Yesterday. A lifetime ago.

Three weak strokes across the pool and her feet found the pebbly bottom. Three more steps and she made it, sprawling across a boulder, panting and coughing away. Her hand still clutched his shirt, and she planned to keep it there for a long, long time.

Tobin flopped on his side, the backpack still in place. He stared at the waterfall.

"Holy shit," he muttered.

She turned and looked at what they'd just done. *Holy shit* pretty much summed it up.

"Are you okay?"

Tobin's eyes held hers. "I'm okay if you're okay."

Everything inside her that was still rattling in shock and fear settled down.

"Okay," she whispered, forcing herself to move. She pulled him up then thumped him on the shoulder for good measure.

Tobin grinned that crooked grin and thumped her right back.

If only it were a day like yesterday. She might just drag him back behind the waterfall for another kiss — or two, or three.

Instead, she looked back up the cliff. "You think those drug runners will follow us down?"

"I think they might."

"And the guides..." she started. "How long would it take them to get back to the village and sound the alarm?"

"Fifteen minutes at a run, maybe."

She nodded. "Plus another half hour to get down here." The hike yesterday had taken them two hours, but that was at a casual pace. If the villagers hoofed it...

"Not very much time."

"Not very much time," she echoed.

"So let's go," Tobin said. His voice was firm, resolute.

She looked at the jungle, crowding in from all sides. "Where to?"

Tobin turned with a devilish grin that only he could pull off at a time like this. His hair was half stuck to his scalp, curling this way and that. A leaf stuck out near his left ear and a line of water trickled down his brow.

Click. She grabbed the moment and stored it away forever. *Knight in shining armor, Tobin-style.*

He reached back, pulled the machete from his backpack, and motioned downslope with it. "Follow me, m'lady."

Chapter Twenty-Four

Tobin stepped through the undergrowth, swinging the machete as he went. He hacked and swore and shoved at the foliage, not that that sped their progress up. Cara followed close enough to keep a hand clutched on his backpack, and he concentrated on that.

Get her out. Must get her out.

Zing! He swung the machete, again and again. *Zing!*

"Can I ask what the rest of the plan is?"

He answered without stopping. "I figure we follow this stream downslope until we hit the trail that runs along the river." *Hopefully.*

That last part, he left out.

They were barely five minutes out of the water and he was already soaked with sweat. He threw another glance over his shoulder, expecting to catch the silent *Pfft!* of a poison dart any second, but there was nothing. Nothing but the mocking sound of a bird, the murmur of the stream.

"And then what?"

"Then we follow that to where I stashed Lucy."

Leaves crunched as Cara pulled up short, her face going red. "Lucy? Who the hell is Lucy?"

Oops. Not the time to get his Italian beauty riled up.

He threw his hands up. "My motorcycle."

The red went back over to pink. "You! You..." She slapped his arm. "Only you would name a motorcycle after a girl!"

"It wasn't me! She was already named when I got her. Julie named her."

"Julie?" She rammed her hands on her hips.

He waved his hands again. "I mean Julie — Seth's girlfriend." He glanced into the rain forest, then grabbed her hand and continued downhill, trying to summarize what had happened in Belize while running full tilt into a spider web of vines. *Serendipity.* Seth and Julie. Illegal artifacts. Sailing, running, saying goodbye.

She stared. "My God, Tobin, what have you been up to over the past couple of months?"

He grinned. If only she knew.

"But how could you trade your grandfather's boat for a motorcycle?" She was steaming now, which made him glow with pride. Few people understood what that boat meant to him, but Cara did. The summers spent sailing on *Serendipity*, the stories his granddad would tell, the dreams he'd encouraged. No way would he ever get rid of that boat.

He couldn't help but wonder what his grandfather would think of him now?

He'd be chuckling at the waterfall escapade, probably, and nodding in approval. But then he'd stare into the distance and tilt his head one way then the other as if there were a crossroads just ahead and he wondered which path Tobin would take.

Tobin wondered, too.

Cara tugged his hand. "I can't believe you gave *Serendipity* away!"

The words jolted him back into the present, and into motion, pulling her along the rough trail. "I didn't! Not really. I mean, it was sort of a trade. Seth and Julie still have the boat. Anyway, it's a long story. Maybe I can tell it to you sometime."

He stopped in his tracks and glanced at Cara. Sometime. Would they ever have that chance?

Her lips quirked a tiny little bit, and a bubble of hope tumbled through him.

"Maybe you can."

They stared at each other until a bird cawed. Time to act, not to wish.

He was just starting to worry that he'd totally miscalculated distances when a hack of the machete brought them to a wide trail with an open view.

"Thank God," he muttered.

"What?" Cara leaned in closer.

He straightened quickly. "Here we are." Because he was supposed to know what he was doing, right? "There's our bridge." He pointed to the graceful arc of the rope bridge to the right.

"That? You call that a bridge?"

He grabbed her hand and set off in the opposite direction at a quick jog.

"But, you just said—" she protested.

"We need Lucy. Shouldn't be far now." He hoped. Because who knew how long they had before they had half the village and six drug runners in hot pursuit?

It was shorter than he thought, and he nearly skidded out in plain view of the bridge guards before grabbing Cara and crouching down. The rope bridge was far behind them now, with the ravine and the new bridge just to the right. The wide road in front of him ran perpendicular to the footpath — the same road to nowhere he'd originally driven up, only to get to the steep incline where he'd stashed his bike.

"Okay, this is the tricky part," he whispered.

"Jumping off the waterfall wasn't the tricky part?"

Good thing she didn't know what he had in mind.

"We have to get around the corner without the guards seeing us to get Lucy." He motioned uphill.

"I thought we're trying to get away from the village, not head back toward it."

"Lucy's not far. Come on!"

He peeked again. No soccer game, by the looks of it. The guards were standing at various corners of the bridge, scanning the scene. Actually paying attention, for a change.

Where was the World Cup when he needed it most?

He edged along the left side of the road, using leaves and vines for cover. A minute later, they padded around the bend and out of sight. Two minutes of puffing uphill to the massive tree trunk he used to remember the spot, and they were there. You couldn't see a thing from the road, but good old Lucy was right where he left her, behind the shed-sized trunk of that tree. Vines were already curling around the wheels — the jungle worked that fast — but a couple of insistent heaves got her free, and with Cara's help, he pushed the aging Kawasaki onto the dirt road.

Cara grabbed his arm. "How are we going to get over the bridge with all those guards there?"

"We're not going over that bridge," he said, handing her the backpack.

"Then what bridge are we going—" Cara went white. "Oh no. Not that bridge. Tell me you're not thinking of that bridge."

A voice rang out from up the road before he could answer, and they whipped their heads toward the source. One voice turned into several as three village men appeared, pointing and hollering and bringing their blowguns to their mouths. Running into view behind them came a couple of the drug-running gang. It was all a blur, but Tobin could tell by the camo. The scrappy beards. The rifles, pointing his way.

"Come on!" he yelled, pushing Lucy down the road. In five steps, they were around the corner and temporarily out of blowgun range — but back in the line of sight of the bridge guards, who still hadn't taken notice of the action. But they would the minute he fired Lucy up, since there wasn't a blaring television adding to the river noise.

Praying the old bike would fire up on the first try, he jumped on, hit the petcock and choke, and threw his weight into the biggest kick start of his life.

Lucy roared, sputtered to a near standstill, and then coughed back to life.

"Get on!" he shouted, pretty much the same second the bridge guards shouted and turned their way.

Cara slid on and he took off so fast, they'd have done a wheelie if it weren't for the downslope. The barrels of several rifles swung their way as he curved left for a clear shot, then right, heading for the narrow riverside path he and Cara had come along minutes earlier.

The rat-a-tat-tat of a rifle sounded. A thousand birds fled the treetops in a giant whoosh. Cara clutched his ribs so hard, he could barely breathe, which was okay since he was barely breathing anyway. Not with a second and third rifle joining in.

He gunned the engine and they shot down the trail with a bump that nearly threw them into the air.

"Oh my God!" Cara screamed.

Yeah, that had been a little closer than he would have liked. But they were hammering down the trail now, and as long as they didn't get guillotined by a low-hanging vine, the twisting path would provide cover from bullets and darts.

"Just hang on!"

He doubted they ever broke thirty, but the foliage blurred by like they were screaming down a highway at a hundred miles an hour. Having Cara on the back threw off the bike's balance, and the number of times he barely averted a wipeout by sticking out a foot... well, he stopped counting.

The rope bridge popped in and out of view, and they shot past the point where he and Cara had slashed their way out of the jungle to join the path. Cara's arms squeezed tighter as he revved to the edge of the rope bridge then stopped. He could feel her weight shift, hear her breath catch as she leaned over his shoulder to see.

"Tobin, are you totally nuts?"

Chapter Twenty-Five

Tobin gulped. The bridge extended before them in a low, elegant curve, dipping down, then climbing up toward the other side. Just like one of those perspective drawings, where everything narrowed on a point on the other side.

A very rickety perspective drawing over a very deep ravine. The roar of the rapids seemed angrier than it had been his first time here, and his stomach churned much like the water one hundred feet below.

The bridge was ridiculously narrow, rickety, and uneven. But it might just work.

Scratch that. It *had* to work.

Cara's fingers tapped on his shoulder, either in prayer or in a silent series of calculations. He felt her haul in a long breath and let it out slowly.

"Ready?" she whispered.

Damn, that was supposed to be his line.

He turned his head and found her obsidian eyes shining at him. It was a look he hadn't seen in a very long time. A look that said *I trust you* and *We're in this together* and *Watch out future, here we come.*

A look he wouldn't mind getting used to seeing every day for the rest of his life.

A giant insect whizzed by his ear, and he ducked.

"Go!" Cara yelled, thumping him on the shoulder. "Go!"

It took him a second to process what she meant, until excited cries filled in behind the sound of the rapids. That wasn't an insect. It was a poison dart. And the men shooting at them were swarming out of the jungle and into easy firing range.

"Go!" Cara screamed.

With a twist of the throttle, they shot across the last two yards of firm ground and hit the first footboard of the bridge. The moment the bike made contact, they dropped a foot before continuing across. The bridge swayed and groaned under the combined weight of Lucy, him, and his Italian princess.

Rat-a-tat-tat! Now rifles were shooting, too. Whether that was the drug runners or the bridge guards, he didn't know. Didn't care what flavor of death found them first. Only wanted to get away.

A nudge between his shoulder blades told him that Cara had hidden her head there. He wished he could do the same — close his eyes and trust someone else to make sure everything came out all right.

But there was no one else. It was all up to him.

All up to him, and Christ, he didn't even trust himself.

He clenched his teeth, forced his eyes wide and somehow kept the bike upright when the bridge went from bending beneath him to flexing back upward. They'd had a cat when he was a kid, a crazy cat who liked being tossed in a blanket. Tobin would hold two corners of the blanket while Seth held the others and they'd launch Mittens into the air like an astronaut hitting zero gravity.

Now he knew how Mittens felt, with two important differences.

The cat loved every minute of it. And cats had nine lives.

What the hell had he been thinking with this insane escape plan?

Pfft! A dart whizzed in front of his face. As if the bouncing bridge weren't enough.

His eyes kept wanting to slide sideways to the cables forming handholds on either side of the bridge. An inch of clearance on either side, max. One little wobble and the handlebars would snag. He could picture it all too easily: the sluggish drag on first contact, the wild swerve he'd put the bike into to pull free. Then he'd tangle with the cable on the other side and get pitched headfirst into the ravine. Him and Cara, flying, flying...

Unless he kept his eyes glued to the far side.

So he kept them glued, religiously, until his eyeballs burned and screamed to blink — just one little blink. But that could be the death of him, and worse, of her. So, no. No blinking allowed.

No blinking, no panicking when the bridge bucked and dipped a lot like his grandfather's boat did when a wave fell away from under the bow and dropped it with a thud. He knew, because there'd been a lot of that when he and Seth sailed down from New England. But that had been thrilling. This was terrifying.

Something pinged. Without looking, he knew it was another dart, plonking off the fuel tank a hair above his thigh. It bounced off his leg before pitching into space and hurtling into the rapids below.

The bike lurched from footboard to footboard, bumping and bouncing and barely staying on course. Any time now, one of the rotting boards would pop and give way.

But they didn't give way, and salvation — the far end of the bridge — kept inching closer and closer. He leaned forward like that would get them there sooner. Cara, too: he could feel her whole body hope, her lips mumbling a prayer against his skin.

Cara. Lips. Prayer.

All up to him.

His subconscious made a thousand dirty deals with the devil. *Get me through this, and I'll give you every Friday night for the rest of my life. Every Saturday morning lie-in, too...*

The list got longer and longer the closer they got to the other side. The devil could have his best pair of carving skis. His surfboard. Hell, the devil could have his firstborn child. Maybe the secondborn, too, especially if the kid turned out anything like the stories his mom told about him—

He brought that train of thought to a screeching halt. The only woman he'd ever want to have kids with was Cara, and there was no way he'd give anything that precious up. Never.

So he rode on through the impossibly narrow slot over an impossibly unstable surface until the front wheel was an inch away from the other side of the ravine. He yanked the handlebars up with everything he had to lift them over the lip between the last footboard and dry earth.

Vrooom! The bike roared away from the swing bridge, running for its life. Gone were the thunder of the rapids, the wobble of the bridge, the blur of the cables left and right. Everything was steady, straight.

Christ. Never in five thousand miles of sailing had landfall been such a relief.

Chapter Twenty-Six

It was ten minutes before Cara worked up the nerve to open her eyes, and another hour before she stopped glancing over her shoulder, watching for the militia she was so sure would appear in hot pursuit. Tobin kept the bike hammering along until the lumpy dirt road joined another that was only very bad, which eventually led to a paved road. That, in turn, spit them out on a highway with a sign that could have said *Heaven*, only it was spelled P-a-n-a-m-a C-u-i-d-a-d. Panama City. She risked a look at her watch as Tobin slalomed the bike around yet another overloaded truck.

She had to look twice and hold her watch against her ear, thinking the waterfall must have busted it. But no, it really was ten a.m. and she really was on her way to the meeting. Even with Tobin pushing the limits like this, though, it would be tight to make it by three. Super tight. The drive out had taken eight hours, and they only had five.

On the other hand, what hadn't been a tight call today? The waterfall, the shooting guards, the rope bridge. Jesus, had they really done all that?

She nearly gave a triumphant whoop when she realized they were clear, until she noticed how white Tobin's knuckles were around the grips.

"Hey," she leaned into his ear and whispered instead of cheering. "We made it."

He slowly shook his head left, then right. "Could have missed."

She barely heard the words over the engine noise, but the layer of muscle bundled around his ribcage had gone all tight. When he exhaled, it was slow and shaky.

"Come on, you've done a hundred risky things in your life." Nothing scared Tobin. Nothing!

"Never with you on the back of my bike."

She could see the thin line of his lips in the sideview mirror. He'd never looked so much like his brother Seth, the serious one.

The next hour must have been the quietest of his life, and hers, too, because everything he'd done for her in the past few days replayed in her mind. The grip she had on his ribs barely eased, though it became a different kind of clutch. The kind that comes from a million regrets and the knowledge that she'd never, ever be able to make it up to him. The only thing she could hope for was forgiveness. A clean slate.

Some example she was, because she hadn't ever offered Tobin that, had she?

She turned her face away from the mirror and closed her eyes.

A long hour later, Tobin clucked at the fuel gage. "We need to make a quick stop."

When he pulled over at a gas station, she felt a hundred years old: stiff and spent and creaky. If Tobin felt the same, he didn't show it. He jumped right off the bike and shot her that trademark smile that had won a thousand women's hearts.

A thousand women, and the only one he wanted was her.

The smile was a little tight, fraying around the edges with worry. He glanced at his watch instead of the cold drinks display. His foot tapped the ground as he waited for the tank to fill.

The man was on a mission, and that mission was her.

"Damn," she murmured when she swung the backpack off. Her things were still in the cheap hotel she'd stayed at before heading to the village a week — an eternity — ago. Well, she could come back for it later, if at all. Everything she needed was right here, anyway.

Tobin, Tobin, and Tobin.

She reached for the outer flap of the backpack and froze.

"What?" His impossibly blue eyes latched onto hers.

She swung the bag around so he could see the dart stuck in it. Right at the top, an inch away from where her neck would have been.

"Christ." He shook his head. "The kids deserve a new roof on the school, but there has to be a better way."

Roof? What roof? "What do you mean?"

"That's what the village was supposed to get in exchange for delaying you. A new roof for the school." Tobin spit on the ground. "Hell of a way to raise money."

She pictured the smiling kids, the friendly women. The patient elders, the clever hunters. Even Rodrigo — they all struck her as good, honest folk. She considered the dart for a good minute, then grabbed a newspaper out of a trash can and wrapped the dart in it. She stashed the whole bundle in a plastic bag and shoved it into the bottom of his backpack. Then she walked to the toilet on shaky feet and washed her hands for a long, long time.

When she came back out, Tobin was leaning on the bike, staring at nothing in particular. A rugged cross between James Dean and Indiana Jones. He looked weary. Worldly. Smoking hot. What the hell had she been thinking to ever let him go?

There was something round and dark in his hand. When he snapped back into focus on her approach and lifted it, she saw what it was. A motorcycle helmet. A brand new, shiny one.

"Come here." He waved her over and slipped it over her head. They stood face to face, neither saying a word as he ran a finger inside, smoothing her hair back with a touch so soft and tender she barely held back a sigh. She closed her eyes, leaned into his hand, and shut out everything in the world but him.

He kissed her, and though his lips were dry and cracked, it still felt like home. A hopeful, almost yearning kiss. For what, she didn't dare wonder. It was another second before Tobin pulled away, and another second before he opened his eyes. When he did, there was a promise in them. That he'd get her where she needed to be. He'd do whatever it took, for her.

Then he pulled his own helmet on — the old one they'd left strapped to the handlebars in the rush of their escape — got on the bike, and nodded toward the road.

"Panama City, here we come."

Chapter Twenty-Seven

A hundred times over the next five hours, Tobin told himself to lighten up and enjoy this beautiful-girl-on-the-back-of-his-bike gig. To enjoy the warmth of Cara pressed up against his back. The comfortable hold of her arms around his waist. The curve of her legs snuggled up behind his.

Except the clock was ticking, and every mile that took them closer to the city was a mile that threatened to drive them further apart.

He hadn't even realized it until now, but the rain forest had slowed time down. He'd been living a fantasy, where Cara was his and he was hers and that was all that mattered. Now they were back in the fast lane — literally — and it felt as if a dozen fingers were snapping at him, hurrying him up. Saying *Come on, hotshot, finish this off.*

The question was, how to finish it off.

You've served your purpose, hotshot. Don't overstay your welcome.

Clearly, Cara appreciated what he'd done. She might even be thinking they might give themselves a second shot, judging by the warm looks and easy touches she gave him. But where would it all lead? The thoughts crowded and tangled in his mind, much like the traffic that built as a jagged city skyline appeared on the horizon. Panama City. A glittering city stuck between the jungle and the sea. From a distance, it looked almost futuristic, but up close, it was a crumbling mess. He'd been through there before heading to Catalina, and once had felt like enough.

Traffic slowed to a crawl when they reached city limits, and he checked his watch. Two o'clock.

"An hour to the presentation," Cara said into his ear.

"You know the way?"

She pointed to a sloping steel high-rise to the right of the others, near but still far. Maybe too far.

He tapped his fingers on the handlebars and cursed the traffic. Didn't matter that it was two o'clock on a Friday and they were heading into the city and not out. In Panama City, the roads were nearly always bumper-to-bumper.

"Screw this." He revved Lucy up and swung into the breakdown lane.

It worked for a while, until the other drivers did the same thing. Another glance at his watch. Two-thirty. Cara's fingers plucked nervously at his shirt, even after he put a hand over hers and squeezed it against his ribs. Which only made the ache in him grow stronger.

Maybe they could stay in traffic all day.

But he'd gotten her this far, damn it. Failure wasn't an option. A man had to have some pride, after all.

He nearly laughed out loud. *Him? Pride?*

But on the other hand... Why the hell not?

He took off through the narrow space between the crawling cars, praying none of them made a sudden lane change. Cara pointed him down one street, then another, and even down one that was closed. He raced around a construction site, flew down a one-way side street, and even a couple of sidewalks before Cara pointed.

"Over there."

He screeched to a stop and parked as Cara spoke rapid-fire Spanish to the guard. Then they were sprinting for the doors. Two fifty-five.

"What floor is it?"

"Sixty-fourth."

Sixty-fucking-four? He pushed the buttons for all the elevators and didn't stop pushing until one of them pinged open and let them in.

The doors closed in a solemn slide. Within two stories of the climb, he was tugging at his shirt collar. For the past couple of days, he'd been outdoors, and even the bungalow they'd slept in felt like a natural extension of the jungle. Now they were in a suffocating metal box on their way to the sixty-fourth floor.

Panama. What a country.

There were mirrors all the way around the elevator, each of them a tease filled with Cara's reflection. She was everywhere, but still too far, so he pulled her close and kissed her for the count of three measured breaths, making the world slow down again. Making him wonder: maybe it wasn't just the jungle that had the magic power to slow things down. Maybe the magic was in the two of them.

The elevator rattled and they broke apart, looking at each other. Her lips twitched like she was going to say something monumental. Something he really, really wanted to hear.

But then the bell pinged. The doors rolled open. It took everything he had not to punch the *Close Door* button to shut them again.

Too late. Cara blinked, stepped out, and strode down the hall.

"God, how do I look?" she murmured, and something in him bubbled with hope, because if she'd missed the mirrors in the elevator, she might have been thinking about him. Maybe even thinking about *them.*

"You look great," he said, plucking a leaf out of her hair. Never mind the mud splattered on her shirt. Cara always looked like a million bucks.

Then they turned a corner and a secretary rushed up to her, whisking Cara toward a glass-walled conference room. Cara only let go of his hand when they got to the very end of their fingertips.

"Will you wait for me? Please?"

He nodded. Of course, he would wait. A hundred years if he had to.

He was about to say as much when a man in a slick Armani suit stepped up, his jaw hanging open. "Cara?"

Her eyes shot daggers at the man. "Surprised to see me, Enrique?"

Enrique? The schmuck who wanted Cara's job? The ass she suspected of holding back the message that she needed help? His fingers closed into two tight fists.

Cara rolled her eyes and strode past the man like he wasn't even worth her time. With a tongue-tied Enrique in tow, she stepped into the conference room. All eyes jumped to her — including the appraising gaze of a couple of men twice her age. Tobin nearly growled aloud. She asked him to stay? He'd stay all right. Right here.

He parked himself on the edge of a plush chair, folded his arms, and did his best to channel *my-woman, keep-your-eyes-and-hands-off* energy through the glass.

She got right to work with a marker, scribbling notes and numbers on a whiteboard. It was like a TV drama, with the glass wall forming an oversized screen. The way she punctuated each argument with insistent chopping motions of her hands, the way her eyes flashed. Hell, if it were him, he'd give her the bid in a heartbeat. And fire that idiot Enrique, who sat hunched in defeat in a corner of the conference room.

But it wasn't up to Tobin who won and who lost. It was up to the suits in there. He hated them already. There was a groomed and styled Latino with poaching eyes. Yeah, that guy wanted Cara. The gray-haired boss looked at her with thinly veiled desire, too. All of them, in fact, looked highly suspicious. She could do better than any of them by a mile.

His soul slumped at the thought that came on the heels of that one. Cara could do better than Tobin Cooper, too.

He spent the next hour contemplating that reality as the meeting dragged on. He would always just be Tobin, and that would never be enough.

Maybe it was time to cut his losses and quit while he was ahead. Because somewhere between the rope bridge and the ping of the elevator, he'd finally figured out what he'd been hoping for over the last couple of days. It wasn't a second chance at Cara or an adventure or even for a night of heaven wrapped around her body, blissful as that was.

It was closure.

Closure on six years of wishing. Wishing to see her smile at him, one more time. To win her trust, even if it was only while hanging off the back of a bike or hurtling off a waterfall. To see her look at him with that special shine lighting up her princess eyes.

And he'd gotten all that. So what was he sticking around for now? Yeah, they loved each other as much — or more — than any two people could. But ultimately, her father was right. Cara could do better.

Unless. . .

He started sifting through the possibilities, hauling out old plans.

The conference room opened, and the babble of voices shook him out of his thoughts. Cara skipped over and smacked into him with a giant hug.

"I did it! We got the bid!"

He couldn't care less about which company won the bid, but he spun her around twice because he'd always cheer for her team. Even if it was filled with a bunch of stuffy-looking assholes in suits.

"That's great!" He kissed her a couple of times, savoring every one.

She rewarded him with a huge smile and a pat on the chest. "It is great. But we have to negotiate a couple of points right now."

"Right now?"

She shrugged. "It's Friday afternoon, and the bigwigs want this settled now. It'll take another hour or two at least."

He shook his head. "No way. You've just crossed half of Panama. Jumped off a waterfall!" Whoa. Had all that really happened today? "You need a break. Food, water." He was babbling, but damn, didn't Cara deserve a break?

She patted his arm. "They're sending food up now. You can snag some off the tray before they bring it in, too. But then I think it makes more sense for you to go to my place and wait there. The secretary can tell you the way."

He didn't want to go anywhere, but her gaze flicked back to the conference room where the suits were watching. Waiting.

"I really have to go." She kissed him and backed away, and it nearly killed him, wondering if that might be the last one. "I'll see you there soon."

He didn't like it, not one bit, but maybe it didn't help to have her seen with a ragged gringo sporting three days of stubble. He looked around until he caught his reflection in a pane of glass. Didn't look any better or worse than usual.

In other words, he stuck out in this office like a sore thumb. He gave himself a little shake, like a dog trying to shed a coat full of burrs.

Cara hurried back into the conference room, blowing him a kiss. "See you soon."

"See you soon," he whispered, wondering if it was a lie.

Chapter Twenty-Eight

Her apartment wasn't far, and with the secretary's directions, Tobin was there in twenty minutes. He swung the door open and peered inside, feeling strangely alone. Three days with Cara and he was already spoiled for life. He sighed and stepped in.

It was one of those modern places where everything was a cool white-on-white. He walked around, feeling like a burglar who wasn't sure what he was looking for. The only comfort was the little hints of Cara filling the corners of the place. The pictures of her family on the fridge. The scrappy college blanket spread across the couch. The picture books arranged neatly on the coffee table.

He scanned them and snorted out loud. *Rain Forests of the World*, said one. He flipped it over and read the back cover. *This stunning visual journey will bring you to the heart of the rainforest and the fascinating cultures that live in harmony with nature...*

Stunning visual journey? It was stunning, all right. His ass still throbbed from the bumps they'd hammered over, because he'd been treated to tactile impressions, too. Not to mention olfactory, because even the stink of the city hadn't purged the rich jungle scent from his memory.

Visual, tactile, olfactory. What else? He rifled through the memories until he screeched to a stop at one.

Sensual. A sensual journey.

They'd had that, too, starting with the kiss under the waterfall and moving on to a night of sexual aerobics in her hut. His eyes strayed to the open door of her bedroom, two steps away. Him and Cara, together again.

His whole body sighed and fast-forwarded through a hundred happy scenarios. Inserted kids and a dog and summer sails on *Serendipity*. Winters on the slopes, autumns full of falling leaves, Halloween costumes, and Thanksgiving feasts. He played them forward, then played them back again. But he kept getting stuck on one scene.

There they were, at a cocktail party to celebrate her company's successful bid, somewhere in the near future. Him and her, cleaned up and looking like a million bucks. Happy as can be until one of the slick suits ambushed him at the bar.

"So, you're Cara's fiancé, huh?" Slick Suit would start, sounding almost-but-not-quite chummy and sincere.

Tobin would stand a little taller and give a little nod, pretending his soul didn't sing every time he heard those two words aimed in his direction. *Cara's fiancé.* He was hers, she was his. Forever.

"Lucky guy," Suit Guy would say, picking his teeth.

Luckiest guy on earth and he knew it, so yeah, he'd give a modest shrug.

And then the assault would begin. Subtly, craftily.

"So, what do you do?"

He'd open his mouth then shut it again, and Suit Guy would smirk. Never mind that Tobin was good at what he did, or proud of what he did. Never mind that it kept him healthy and happy. That it made him money, too — more than the average person would guess. None of that counted for anything, though, not in Cara's world. He'd always be the ski bum. Never good enough.

Cara would come over just in time to rescue him, but it always started and ended the same way — with Suit Guy seeing him off with a look that said, *She deserves someone better. Someone like me.*

He could imagine the scene perfectly because it had played out exactly that way a dozen times in the past when they really were engaged. It shouldn't bother him, but it did. What if a couple of years slipped by and she started to think the same thing?

He looked out the window, where a dozen freighters waited their turn to transit the Panama Canal. Ships in limbo between two seas.

Every part of his body screamed for him to go soak in the shower, then crash among the dozen pink throw pillows on her bed and tune out until she woke him up with a kiss and slid in beside him. A fantasy that almost won him over there and then.

There was another fantasy, though, alongside that one. One in which he never had to wonder if he was good enough for her again.

He scrubbed a hand over his face. Doing the right thing had a way of burning a guy, even when he had the best intentions. He'd proved that again and again. Chances were ninety-nine to one he'd lose her again — maybe even to one of those jerks in a suit. Because why would Cara want to wait for him?

He stared off into the boundless blue Pacific, wondering. Then he sat down at her desk, weary to the bone.

He slid a drawer open, knowing what he had to do to make this a start rather than an end. Knowing that the hardest part was still to be done. Harder than sleeping next to her without touching. Harder than jumping off a waterfall or riding across a rope bridge.

Writing the letter he had to write was harder than all that. And leaving would be the hardest part of all.

As he pulled out her stationery and stared at the blank page, his mind tortured him with images of what would happen after he left. The door would swing open and Cara would walk in, calling his name brightly, eager to share her triumph. She'd walk from room to room looking for him, and it shredded him to think how much it would hurt her to find him gone.

But if he didn't do this now, he might never have the nerve to do it again.

He lowered the pen to the paper and began to write.

Dear Cara. . .

Epilogue

New England, four months later...

Cara held up the lavender paper, reading the lines for the thousandth time.

Dear Cara,

Please believe me when I say that leaving is the last thing I want to do...

She lowered it again to keep her eyes on the icy ground but let the words play on in her mind. She had them memorized by now, anyway, and played the letter back like a recording as her boots crunched over the packed snow of the parking lot.

But I need to do this, just like you needed to get to your meeting in time.

The meeting she'd come home from, ready to beg Tobin to stay, only to find him gone.

I never stopped loving you, Cara, and I never will. But I think you were right. We weren't ready to get married back then. And even though I want to meet you at your door with a bottle of champagne and a ring and a promise, I think we're still not ready...

That part of the letter hurt the most because she'd been so sure that after everything they'd been through, things would be all right.

I need a little time to set some things up.

That was the hook that kept her baited over the next couple of lines, which were full of cross-outs. *If you love me...* The latter two words were crossed out and replaced by *If you believe me,* which he'd crossed out in turn before settling on something else: *trust me.*

151

If you trust me...

Trust. She knew he wasn't pointing the finger there, though he had every right to do just that. It was her who'd ruined everything their first time around by not trusting him. Her, who'd driven him away.

If you trust me, and trust that this crazy force field that starts up between us whenever we're together can wait just a little longer...

When she'd first read the next lines, she'd been crushed to read that he wasn't asking for days, but months. She'd already gone forever without him, only to live a lifetime in a couple of days. Waiting four months felt like death, but how could she not wait?

So she waited as long as she could — three months and twenty-six days, not that she'd been counting — and here she was, just as directed in the letter.

She looked down at the address he'd written, then up again. Beech Tree Hill.

A ski slope. A little tiny one.

It looked like a farm had been converted to a modest ski hill, with a quaint old barn that oozed New England warmth on this crisp winter day. It wasn't a big place, but there was a nice vibe to it. Lots of happy kids and proud parents bubbling with good cheer, all of them winding down at what seemed to be the end of a busy day.

A sign over one door said *Office*, and the one next to it, *Ski School.*

Ski school. Surely she'd find Tobin there, right?

A bell jingled as she opened the door then waited as a young mother herded her children toward the desk. "Today was great! Is there any space in beginner lessons next week?"

"All booked, sorry," the young man said. "But I can put you on the waiting list."

The woman sighed, added her name to the list, and bundled her kids off.

"Can I help you?" the young man asked Cara. His eyes seemed to spend an extra minute analyzing her face, and she figured it was the tan.

Panama, she wanted to say. *Just flew in.* But she got right to the point instead. "I'm looking for Tobin Cooper, please."

He flicked a thumb up. "Next door. That way."

So she went back out and up the stairs to the office, wondering what business Tobin might have there.

The barn looked ramshackle from the outside, but it was newer and fresher the higher up she climbed. One story up, a sign pointed right, to the office. The staircase continued upward, but that part was cordoned off. *Private.*

She turned right, followed a short hallway, and peered into the office. The door was open, and she stared for a minute at the view. Two walls of the office were taken up by panoramic windows: one side overlooking the bustling slope, the other capturing a quiet scene of bucolic farms and wooded hills that stretched to distant mountains. Her breath caught, it was so beautiful. So different than the saturated greens of Panama. The wood-burning stove glowing in one corner made her wonder about the apartment upstairs. It had to be gorgeous up there, under the eaves.

She was about to rap on the open door when she saw the sign there. *OWNER*, said a dusty old plate.

Tobin Cooper, said the shiny new plate underneath.

Her knees wobbled just a little bit.

I need a little time to set some things up, he'd written in his letter, and sweet Jesus, it sure looked like he had.

The office walls were hung with pictures of young skiers. She looked from face to smiling face. Not one showed Tobin tearing down the slopes, or Tobin on the podium after winning yet another race. He'd won plenty in his time, but what was he showing off in his office? Joy. Youth. Happiness.

A little bit of Tobin was in every one of those pictures. And something else, too: pride.

She was still gaping at it all when the floorboards shifted behind her and a man spoke.

"Can I help you?"

She spun to face the stranger and mumbled for a minute before producing coherent words. "I'm here to see Tobin."

He looked her up and down. "He's outside. Can I help you?"

"I need Tobin." Part of her winced at how that sounded, but heck, it was true. "I'll wait."

Wait? her body cried. She couldn't wait another second.

It must have shown, because the man sighed and pointed down the stairs. "Follow me."

Her heart beat faster with every step down the winding stairs and outside into the frosty air. The sun was dropping fast, bathing the snowy hills in pink. A crowd gathered at the bottom of the slope, huddled around a three-step podium grand enough for the winter Olympics. Each step was crowded with little red-cheeked girls wearing tiny medals around their necks.

"A big hand for the contestants in today's under-ten girls' event!" A familiar voice announced, and Cara stopped in her tracks.

There was applause, the flash of a dozen cameras, a ripple of approval from the crowd, but all she saw was Tobin.

Tobin, in his white ski parka and jeans. A microphone in his hand, a smile glowing on his face. The kind of smile you get from giving, not taking.

"Hey, Tob." The man tugged on his sleeve.

"One second."

"Um, Tobin," the man tried again.

"Not now, Gus."

"Tobin, I really think—"

Tobin turned to Gus, who flicked a thumb over his shoulder, pointing at her. Tobin's eyes followed the thumb and turned to wide fields of blue.

He froze, and she did, too, because seeing him here wiped her brain clean of all the words she'd wanted to say. She had the vague sense of a hundred pairs of curious eyes swinging in her direction, but the only gaze she cared about was his.

Tobin, looking at her like he'd won the Olympics, and she was the prize. Except this time, his reaction said he didn't even know he'd been in the running. His Adam's apple bobbed in a massive gulp.

There was a jangle as Gus took the remaining medals out of his hand. "I got this, man," he said, sotto voice. Gus shoved Tobin her way, then turned to the audience, raising his voice. "Right, folks! On to the next event. Calling all under-ten boys to the podium..."

She didn't catch the rest, because Tobin came stumbling toward her. Tobin, stumbling — that had to be a first. Her arms opened to catch him, and the next thing she knew, he was wrapped around her like a cape, his arms cinched as tightly as she'd once held him on the back of the bike.

The dead of winter in New England, cold enough for their breath to come out in swirling white puffs, but all she felt was warmth. Warmth and a pulsing kind of joy. Tobin clutched her, her head under his chin, nose to his chest, and he smelled so familiar, so good. She clung to him, making a thousand silent vows. To never doubt, to never leave again.

He made a little croaking sound and led her away from the crowd, up a little rise surrounded by trees.

"You came," he said, holding her shoulder as if to assure himself she really was there.

"You'd have come for me. You did come for me."

"You waited," he said between two uncertain breaths.

She laughed, not too convincingly. "That was the hard part."

You trusted, his eyes said, and when she dipped her head in a nod, he pulled her back into a hug.

"Tobin," she started when he let her go. But her tongue couldn't quite find the right words, so she rooted in her pocket, pulled out a card, and handed it to him.

Even in the dim light, she could see his eyes shine in recognition. It was his card to her — his proposal, from all those years ago.

A year ago we met on this very mountain and you changed my life. I'll love you forever, Cara. Will you be mine?

The card was frayed and warped from their wild escape, but the words were still there, along with her answer.

Yes, Tobin, yes. I'll be yours forever.

She'd added a little more underneath, and her heart was in her throat as his eyes slowed to read it.

Second try, she'd written in. *I'll love you forever, Tobin. Will you be mine?*

It wasn't the same mountaintop and it wasn't Valentine's day. She hadn't organized a candlelight dinner, but somehow, it felt even more right now than it had back then.

His eyes shot up to hers, and the blue of his eyes was fierce. "I've always been yours, Cara."

She more or less threw herself at him then and mumbled into his shoulder. "I know. I'm sorry. For everything."

He put his forehead against hers and spoke so quietly, she could barely hear. "I'm not."

Another little bit of Tobin wisdom. The more she thought about it, the more she knew he was right. For all the regret, the pain, the empty years, they'd earned it this time. Earned each other and their happiness. Because that's all she could see from where she stood to the horizon: a lifetime of happiness with her man.

"I mean it, you know," she sniffed, brushing a mitten across her cheek. "Be mine, as in, all the way."

"I mean it, too." Then he flashed one of his trademark naughty grins. "I wonder how long marriage licenses are good for in this state?"

He might have been joking, or might not have been, but she sure wasn't. "I checked. Sixty days, so our old one is expired. But the nearest office is ten miles away, and it opens at nine in the morning."

His eyebrows shot up and he tilted his head right then nodded slowly. "You have done your homework."

"I've had a lot of time to plan." And hope, and fret.

He clapped in an all-right-then motion. "Great! We can get married tomorrow." His voice was light, but he was studying her reaction like he still wasn't sure she meant it.

She meant it all right, but there was a catch.

"Unfortunately, there's a three-day waiting period after you apply."

He blinked. "Wow. You really have done your homework." Then he shook his head. "Like after waiting six years they think I need to think this over?"

She laughed aloud, and it felt good. Great. Liberating.

"More like, after six years, I think we can survive three more days."

"Not so sure," he pouted and reeled her back in.

She snuggled up against him. "Just think of all the catching up we can do in three days."

His mouth curled up. "I like the sound of that."

"Of course, we do need to figure out a couple of things."

He eyed her suspiciously. "Like what?"

"Like how we're going to get this to work." She waved a hand over the ski slopes, then in the vague direction of the Boston suburb where her new assignment was.

"Simple," he shrugged. "We just make it work."

Typical Tobin. But he was right. They would make it work. And really, how hard could it be? When she'd turned down the promotion she'd been offered on the heels of the successful deal in Panama and asked for a transfer back to the US office instead, she'd insisted on two things. A three-week break before she started working again, and a flex-time arrangement where she was only required to be in the office every second week. Because work wasn't everything in life. At least, she hoped it didn't have to be.

One week out of two in the office. The rest of the time, she would work from home.

Home. She'd been hoping home would be wherever Tobin was, but this… Her eyes swept over the view. The barn, the hills, the snow. This was all an unexpected bonus.

So that part was easier than she thought. What else was on the list? Oh, yes. "Anyway, we can use the three days to plan our shotgun wedding…"

"Whatever you want, it's fine with me." He nodded like a gleeful puppy. "It's perfect."

"We have to plan our honeymoon, too." She looked over the bustling scene. "Once ski season is over, I guess."

"Honeymoon?" He laughed. "If you say Panama, I'll—"

She put a hand to his lips, and he kissed it right away. "Definitely not Panama. Somewhere else. But somewhere warm for sure."

He smiled and though the winter sun was getting low, it felt like summer had hit their section of the mountain.

"Preferably a place with no poison darts," he said.

"Oh!" Her hands started to flutter as she remembered just how much catching up they had to do. "The darts weren't poison."

He tilted his head.

"I had them tested. They were coated with a strong sedative, but not the really potent stuff."

He snorted. "Would have been potent enough if they'd hit us on the bridge."

She shook her head. "The lab said it was slow-acting stuff. We'd have fallen off Lucy a mile or so down the road, but not on the bridge."

"Why are you siding with them, anyway?"

Her chest went all warm, the way it always did when she thought about Tucumba. "Because I think Rodrigo and the rest of them are genuine people. Well, everyone but Lefebvre and his buddies. And the TeleCel guys who made the initial trip out to the village — Enrique and some others — are real jerks. I bet they stepped on a lot of toes. No wonder the villagers wanted the other company to win the bid."

He pulled his lips into a tight line, considering. "So you're saying you work for the bad guys?"

She let a smile out. "Not so bad after all. I talked them into a bonus payment for the village. The school got its new roof, plus a lot of supplies."

His eyes slid over to the kids being bundled off the slope and nodded slowly. "Nice."

"And you want to know the bonus?"

"Bonus?"

"The government insisted on beefing up patrols in the area to protect the new satellite dish, so maybe Tucumba won't have to deal with those drug runners any more."

He smiled. "That is good." Then he scowled. "Then they only have that ass of an anthropologist, Lefebvre, to deal with."

She shook her head. "Apparently, he left. Heading for the Amazon jungle. New cultures to study."

"Right," Tobin scoffed. "With new types of drugs to get him high."

"Whatever." She waved a hand. "It's all good."

"It is good."

Tobin's smile seemed to reach inside her and turn on every bulb. Yes, it was good. A good feeling to be part of it, too.

"But hey, don't get me off the subject. We were planning our honeymoon."

His eyes lit up. "How about a little east of Panama?"

East? "How far east?"

"Saint Lucia, maybe?"

"What's in Saint Lucia?"

"You mean other than gorgeous Caribbean beaches and coconut-husk drinks?" Tobin laughed before growing serious. "There's *Serendipity*." He said it reverently, like his grandfather's boat wasn't just a boat but a family heirloom. Which in a way, it was.

"I thought your cousins Mia and Meredith got to sail it next."

His whole body seemed to smile. "They did. I mean, they are. Meredith is bringing the boat there now."

"Meredith?"

"Yup, she and her new boyfriend. And wait 'til you hear what happened to them."

"Wait — I thought she swore off relationships since..." She trailed off, avoiding the subject. "Since you-know-what. Meredith has a boyfriend now?"

He chuckled. "Meredith found herself a guy in Grenada — a good guy."

"Go, Mer!" Part of her gave a big cheer. If anyone deserved happiness, it was Meredith.

Tobin nodded. "According to my mother, it's downright scandalous. I say, about time Meredith had a little fun. She deserves it."

"Who is this guy? What happened? And what about Mia?"

He laughed. "What happened to Mia is even crazier. She was scuba diving in Bonaire when..." He trailed off and put a finger to her lips. "A story for another time. Meredith is heading for Saint Lucia now, and I bet we can get *Serendipity* for a week or two when they finish up." He slung an arm around her shoulder and swept a hand over the western horizon. "Just think. A winter here. You and me, curled up in front of the fireplace..."

"Fireplace?" She snuggled in closer.

He kissed the top of her head and looked toward the top floor of the barn. "Wait 'til I show you."

So he wasn't kidding her. She was already picturing the sweet little apartment there. Cozy as cozy could be.

"We spend the winter here," he continued, "then set off on our next tropical adventure. A short one, at least. I've got business commitments, you know."

His joking tone didn't fool her because he stood straight as he said it. And yes, she'd be proud, too, if she were him. Heck, *she* was proud of him. Prouder than she'd ever been.

She breathed in and out, in perfect time with him. Maybe that was the key to happiness. Finding pride and joy in something other than yourself.

Click, went her mental camera, one more time. No caption on this one. Just the sketch of a heart with their initials inside.

She pulled him in for a full-body hug and a kiss. "I'm not so sure about the adventure part. The only adventure I want is a life with you." He smiled against her lips, and she snuggled closer. His heat was reaching out to her, and she'd had enough talking for now.

"Now tell me, hotshot," she finished. "How far is that fireplace?"

∞∞∞∞

A note from the author

I hope you've enjoyed your adventure in Panama! Before you check your map or contact your travel agent, let me come clean with the facts. While there really are tiny rain forest villages where indigenous people hold out against the onslaught of "civilization" (most of them every bit as hospitable as those in the fictional hamlet of Tucumba), most prefer to be left in peace. Some leaders are every bit as passionate as Rodrigo about protecting their traditional way of life. Most visitors never get to see this side of the country, sticking instead to Panama City, the canal zone, or the coasts. But even in these "tamer" areas, you'll be fascinated by the wild landscape and cultural melting pot that is Panama. I sure was in the months I spent there!

Sneak Peek: Windswept

She's in deep — in love and in trouble. Scuba instructor Mia Whitman has traveled to Bonaire to forget, not forgive, the man who broke her heart. But trouble is brewing in this Caribbean island paradise — above and below the waterline. When Mia witnesses a crime, she becomes a target, and even she has to admit that having a Navy-SEAL-turned-New-York-City-cop at her side has its perks. Ryan Hayes has a knack for saving her life and stealing her heart — a tricky combination for a woman on the run. Before Mia can stop herself, she finds herself in deep — in love and in trouble.

Books by Anna Lowe

Serendipity Adventure Romance

Off the Charts

Uncharted

Entangled

Windswept

Adrift

Travel Romance

Veiled Fantasies

Island Fantasies

Spellbound in Sedona

Wind Whisperer (Book 1)

Fire Dancer (Book 2)

Dream Weaver (Book 3)

Sherwood Forest Shifters

Tempting the Sheriff (Book 1)

Tempting the Outlaw (Book 2)

Tempting the Maiden (Book 3)

Aloha Shifters - Jewels of the Heart

Lure of the Dragon (Book 1)

Lure of the Wolf (Book 2)

Lure of the Bear (Book 3)

Lure of the Tiger (Book 4)

Love of the Dragon (Book 5)

Lure of the Fox (Book 6)

Aloha Shifters - Pearls of Desire

Rebel Dragon (Book 1)

Rebel Bear (Book 2)

Rebel Lion (Book 3)

Rebel Wolf (Book 4)

Rebel Heart (A prequel to Book 5)

Rebel Alpha (Book 5)

Fire Maidens - Billionaires & Bodyguards

Fire Maidens: Paris (Book 1)

Fire Maidens: London (Book 2)

Fire Maidens: Rome (Book 3)

Fire Maidens: Portugal (Book 4)

Fire Maidens: Ireland (Book 5)

Fire Maidens: Scotland (Book 6)

Fire Maidens: Venice (Book 7)

Fire Maidens: Greece (Book 8)

Fire Maidens: Switzerland (Book 9)

The Wolves of Twin Moon Ranch

Desert Hunt (the Prequel)

Desert Moon (Book 1)

Desert Blood (Book 2)

Desert Fate (Book 3)

Desert Heart (Book 4)

Desert Rose (Book 5)

Desert Roots (Book 6)

Desert Destiny (Book 7)

Sasquatch Surprise (Book 8)

Desert Yule (a short story)

Desert Wolf: Complete Collection (Four short stories)

Blue Moon Saloon

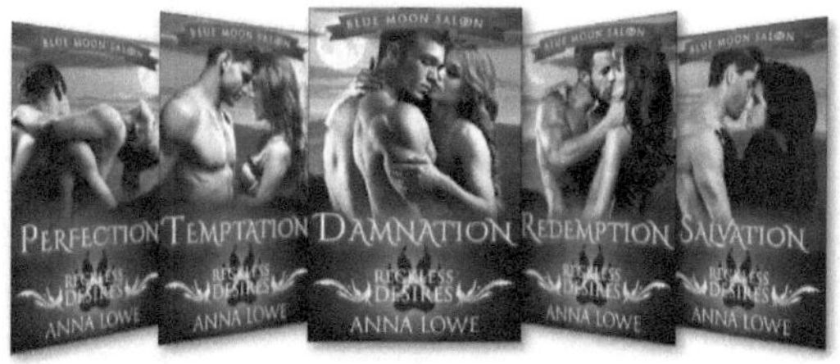

Perfection (a short story prequel)

Damnation (Book 1)

Temptation (Book 2)

Redemption (Book 3)

Salvation (Book 4)

Deception (Book 5)

Celebration (a holiday treat)

Shifters in Vegas

Paranormal romance with a zany twist

Gambling on Trouble

Gambling on Her Dragon

Gambling on Her Bear

Gambling on Her Panther

www.annalowebooks.com

About the Author

USA Today and Amazon bestselling author Anna Lowe loves putting the "hero" back into heroine and letting location ignite a passionate romance. She likes a heroine who is independent, intelligent, and imperfect – a woman who is doing just fine on her own. But give the heroine a good man – not to mention a chance to overcome her own inhibitions – and she'll never turn down the chance for adventure, nor shy away from danger.

Anna loves dogs, sports, and travel – and letting those inspire her fiction. On any given weekend, you might find her hiking in the mountains or hunched over her laptop, working on her latest story. Either way, the day will end with a chunk of dark chocolate and a good read.

Visit *AnnaLoweBooks.com*